THE METHUSELAH METHOD

BARBARA WALKER

Copyright © 2018 Barbara Walker
All rights reserved
First Edition

PAGE PUBLISHING, INC.
New York, NY

First originally published by Page Publishing, Inc. 2018

ISBN 978-1-64214-454-3 (Paperback)
ISBN 978-1-64214-455-0 (Digital)

Printed in the United States of America

Altogether, Methuselah lived 969 years, and then he died.
—*Genesis 28:5*

Alchemy: an early form of chemistry, with philosophic and magical associations, studied in the middle ages; its chief aims were to change base metals into gold and to discover the elixir of perpetual youth.

Elixir: (1) a substance sought by medieval alchemists because it was thought to have the power to change base metals into gold or to prolong life indefinitely. (2) a supposed remedy for all ailments.

*****

The search for the secret to youth and longevity is an ancient one. Many medieval practitioners of alchemy pursued the legendary "elixir of life" or "elixir of immortality," as it was also called. It is a mythical potion that grants the drinker eternal life or eternal youth. Its basis is "white gold." The ancient scholar and German abbot, Trithemius (1462–1516), on his deathbed, dictated a recipe that he said would preserve mind, health, and memory, with perfect sight and hearing for those who made use of it. It consisted of, among other things, calomel, gentian, cinnamon, aniseed, coral, nard, tartar, and mace. Five grams of it were to be taken morning and night in wine during the first month; during the second month, it was to be taken in the morning only; during the third month three times a week, and so on throughout life.

The myth of the "fountain of youth" dates back more than three thousand years and spans cultures and continents. It has been placed in the Americas, Asia, Ethiopia, and once was named for the Amazon River. The explorer, Juan Ponce de León, was said to have been searching for the fountain when he discovered the state of Florida.

In more recent times, in the 1970s, scientists discovered an agent (the antifungal rapamycin) produced by soil bacteria on Easter Island that they claim has life-extending properties. One study is said to have shown an increase in the life expectancy of rats: males by 28 percent and females by 38 percent.

Nowadays, in the twenty-first century, although we are living longer, we still hate growing older. We no longer believe in the concept of "growing old gracefully"; we just don't want to grow old—period. There was a time when it was mainly women who wanted to erase the signs and symptoms of advancing age. Now, men too have jumped on the bandwagon. Look at the success of Viagra. Isn't that just an attempt to turn back a man's sexual clock to what he believes was a better place and time? Humankind has become more and more preoccupied with so-called antiaging products and processes. There are literally thousands of products on the market that are advertised as having the ability to make us look, feel, and function better. Is there really a way to turn back nature's clock—to actually reverse the aging process? Modern expectations are on a highly touted and very expensive product called HGH, a human growth hormone, which some doctors call antiaging, regenerative, or age-management medicine. Is it the modern-day fountain of youth? Does it work? In the opinion of many health professionals, you would be better served by investing in methods to maintain your health and body; proper weight control, diet, exercise, nonsmoking, preventive health care, etc. But who's to say for sure—what if someone actually could unlock the secret of youth and longevity? Would such a discovery be the pot of gold at the end of the rainbow, or would it open a Pandora's box of new evils for those who would take advantage of a gullible population?

CHAPTER 1

The noise in Barbara's ears was practically driving her crazy. It had started out a few weeks ago as a "whooshing" sound, and now it had escalated into a shrill ringing like a fire engine siren passing by on the street outside her house. At least that's what she thought until she cracked open her eyes and realized that the sound was the ringing of the telephone on her bedside table; that's what had awakened her out of a deep sleep. The ringing stopped before she could pick up the phone. She glanced at the number on the caller ID and realized that it was from Maryann, her godchild and the daughter of her lifelong best friend, Marigold Robbins. She glanced at the digital clock sitting next to the phone. The big red LCD readout said 6:31. Alarm bells started go to off in her head. Why was Maryann calling so early in the morning? Barbara swung her feet to the floor and sat there for a minute or two so that her blood pressure could stabilize. She had learned that you must do that stuff when you're old and have hypertension, diabetes, and the like. Taking a deep breath, she picked up the phone and pressed the appropriate buttons to call Maryann back. She answered on the first ring.

"Maryann," she chided, "you know I love you dear, but it's a little early for a wake-up call."

"Hello, Ms. Barbara," she said. "I'm sorry to bother you so early, but I'm a little worried about Mother."

"That's okay, honey, I was about to get up anyway," Barbara replied, which was a lie, but hey, what's the difference, she thought. "What's wrong with Marigold?"

"That's just it," said Maryann. "I don't know that anything's wrong, but I also don't know where Mother is. I've been calling both her landline and cell phone numbers since around five o'clock yesterday evening, and she doesn't answer. I thought she might be at your house—you know, maybe you guys had a sleepover or something."

"A sleepover … I haven't had one of those since I was twelve years old, and no, I haven't seen Marigold since—oh, let me see—it was Wednesday when we went to the mall and spent half our social security checks at the Coach store buying designer purses we don't even need. Did you check with the phone company to make sure her land line is working? You know we had those high winds yesterday. I saw on the news that some people lost power. Maybe her cell phone is out of juice, and she can't charge it up if her house power it out."

"No, her house phone isn't out. I already checked with the phone company. I don't know what I should do, Ms. Barbara," said Maryann, and it was evident from her tone of voice that she was really worried. "I called her next-door neighbor—you know, that nosy Mrs. Adams who sees everything that goes on in the entire block—and she says Mother's Lexus is parked in the driveway, but she didn't see the porch light come on last night. I hate to ask you, Ms. Barbara, but could you go over there and make sure Mother hasn't had a stroke or fallen down or something? I know you have that extra key to her house, and it would take me two hours to drive down there, besides which, if there's nothing wrong, Mother will give me a tongue-lashing that I won't forget for days. You know how independent she is and doesn't like me to hover over her. I'm trying not to overreact, but if you can't go check on her, then I'll have to call the police." The alarm bells in Barbara's head began to get louder, and she felt a little sick to her stomach. She and Marigold had been friends their entire lives—literally—their mothers met in the hospital the day they were born within two hours of each other, with Barbara being the older. They had been inseparable when they were growing up and had lived within fifty miles of each other their entire lives, except when they were in college; Barbara at the University of Virginia and Marigold at Carnegie-Mellon. The thought that something bad had happened to Marigold filled her with a deep dread. But she tried to put a good spin on it for Maryann's sake. "Honey, don't panic, I'm sure Marigold is okay, but I'm going to get dressed and go over there as soon as you hang up. You keep calling her phone numbers, and if she answers, call me on my cell."

"Oh, thank you so much, Ms. Barbara," said Maryann. "I'm hanging up now so you can get dressed. I am so on pins and needles here." The phone beeped in her ear as she hung up.

Barbara threw on a pair of sweats that she had discarded on the floor the night before, shoved her feet into a pair of scuffed-up running shoes, grabbed her keys and purse, and ran out the door. She didn't take time to bother with personal hygiene. Her heart was beating a mile a minute, and she pushed the speed limit as she drove the ten miles from her apartment to Marigold's house. All the while she was keeping up a conversation with herself inside her head. "Oh, Marigold, please be all right. Please be all right. I don't know what I would do if something happened to you. Please be all right."

Even as early as it was, the nosy neighbor across the street pushed her curtains aside to peer out as Barbara pulled into the driveway behind Marigold's brand-new gold Lexus. She scrambled through the junk in her purse until she found the key to Marigold's house and tried to remember the alarm code before she unlocked the door. She hoped the numbers were right—at sixty-six years old, her memory was not what it used to be, and she sure didn't want to have to contend with the alarm company if she couldn't shut the thing off. She unlocked the door and was momentarily surprised that the alarm did not start beeping. It apparently wasn't even set. That was definitely not like Marigold—she never went to bed without turning the damn thing on. "Goldie," yelled Barbara as she stepped into the house "Are you here?" Nothing but silence answered. Fearfully, she went from room to room on the lower level. Everything was in its place—except Marigold, that is; she was nowhere to be found. She tried to slow the hammering of her heart as she climbed the stairs to the second level of the house, almost sick with dread, afraid of finding her best friend in the world badly hurt, dead, or dying. The bathroom door was open, the room was spick-and-span as usual, and Marigold was not there. The guest bedroom door was also open—again, no Marigold. Taking a deep breath, Barbara pushed opened the master bedroom door, certain that disaster awaited inside. The room was immaculate, the bed still made, but Marigold was not there. Just then, she heard her cell phone ringing from inside her purse, which was, of course, downstairs on the coffee table where she had thrown it when she first came into the house. She ran downstairs, rummaged through the cluttered purse, and answered it before it stopped ringing. As she suspected, it was Maryann. "Is she there, Ms. Barbara, is she hurt?" Maryann blurted out, her tone indicating that she was expecting bad news.

"Here's the thing, Maryann, your mother is not here. Her bed is made up, like it hasn't even been slept in. Maybe she had a date last night and just stayed over with a man friend. You know she's been doing that eHarmony thing on the Internet, trying to find a companion to spend some time with. If she's with a guy, that's probably why she didn't answer her cell phone." As she said those words to Maryann, Barbara knew in her heart that they just didn't ring true. Marigold never, absolutely never, turned her cell phone off. *And as sure as I'm living and breathing*, Barbara thought, *if Goldie was going out with a man, she would have told me. We tell each other everything—even those things we won't tell our children or even our pastor. That's how close a relationship we have with each other.*

"What are you saying, Ms. Barbara?" said Maryann, with even more alarm in her voice. "Are you saying that Mother was trying to find a date online? She knows that stuff is dangerous. There are perverts and all kinds of freaks out there. I can't believe my mother would do a thing like that. She's too intelligent. She has a PhD in psychology, for God's sake. She knows better."

Barbara understood the young woman's reaction. Maryann was a single mother, raising a six-year-old daughter, Amber. At twenty-nine years of age, with a failed marriage and a divorce under her belt, she was understandably somewhat embittered toward men in general and toward her ex-husband, Andrew, in particular. After her dad died, Maryann—in reversal of the traditional mother-daughter role—began to caution Marigold against "hooking up with some jerk" who would take advantage of someone her age. Marigold was irritated, but she took her daughter's protestations for what they were, a well-intentioned, but overly aggressive, attempt at taking care of her mother as any caring daughter would.

Barbara realized that Maryann just didn't have a clue. She had been married for two short years. She couldn't know about the loneliness a woman feels when the husband she spent most of her life with up and dies on her, like Marigold's Melvin did three years ago—like her Herman did just two years ago. She didn't know how you miss being held in someone's arms and loved. She didn't realize that you miss sex even when you're in your sixties. And she didn't realize that all the usual, so-called safe, forums for meeting people just don't work anymore when you're over sixty. All the men at church are either married or too old or interested in younger women. There are always twice as many women than men at the ballroom dancing halls. Senior citizens don't frequent bars much anymore. So, where do you look for companionship and affection when you crave it?

"Look, Maryann, I know this is hard for you, but like you said, your mother is intelligent. She wouldn't do anything incredibly stupid, like meeting someone she hadn't checked out thoroughly. You know yourself, she is very, very good at using the Internet. We're going to have to be patient and wait until she calls—and she will call, I'm certain of it. As a matter of fact, she and I are scheduled to go to our golf banquet at one o'clock today. She wouldn't miss that for the world because she's sure that she's going to get a trophy for the tournament this year."

"I don't know, Ms. Barbara," said Maryann. "I think we should call the police."

"And tell them what, Maryann, that a grown woman, an old grown woman at that, didn't go home last night and is not answering her cell phone? There is nothing amiss at her house. She wasn't carjacked because her car is parked in the driveway. Besides, I don't think the police will even start looking for someone until they're missing for over twenty-four hours. What time did you start trying to call her yesterday?"

"It was about five o'clock in the evening," said Maryann. "I wanted to tell her about my new job. She told me to call her as soon as I found out, and that she'd be waiting to hear from me."

"And it's what now, seven thirty," said Barbara. "That's only about fourteen hours or so. I don't think the police would even take a report at this point. If Marigold doesn't show up for the banquet, or call me by that time, then I'll go to the police with you, okay. But stop worrying so much, your mother's a big girl, capable of taking care of herself, like she's always done. Don't think yourself into an anxiety attack. I don't want you to have to be rushed to the emergency room."

"I'll try not to be so panicky, Ms. Barbara," said Maryann. "But I've got a bad feeling about this, a very bad feeling. It's just not like Mother to be out of touch like this—she's never done that before. She knows how paranoid I am."

After she hung up with Maryann, Barbara had to sit down for a minute to try to calm herself down. She didn't believe a word that she had said to Maryann but knew it was true that the police wouldn't take a report seriously at this point. Her oldest son was a police investigator, so she knew the drill. Her heart was going like a trip-hammer, and she realized that she had rushed off without taking her blood pressure pills. A tingling sensation traveling up her spine was a sure indicator that her blood pressure was high. She stared at her cell phone like it was alive. "Please call me, Goldie," she implored. "Please call." Of course, the darn thing stayed silent. Just then, she realized that she was a very poor detective. She hadn't checked the basement or the garage. In the crime novels, she read—and she read them by the ton—you should check everywhere. She went down into the basement, which Goldie always insisted on calling the "lower level" because it was completely furnished and as luxurious as some exclusive apartments. Barbara found nothing out of the ordinary. *Marigold is the neatest person I have ever known*, she thought. *Probably obsessive-compulsive. Nothing could ever be out of place.* She stepped out of the side door into the attached garage. Barbara almost laughed at how tidy the space was. Even the floors looked scrubbed. Again, everything appeared as it should be. Barbara was perplexed and very, very worried.

She decided to have one more look around upstairs before leaving, this time even getting down on the floor and looking under the beds. Nothing under either one, not even dust bunnies. She opened the walk-in closet and found two things that were out of place. Marigold's new designer purse, the black-and-brown Coach she had bought at the mall last Wednesday, was nowhere to be found, and her Gucci overnighter was also not in the closet. She then checked the closet in the guest bedroom. Neither item was there. "Marigold, you stinker," she said to herself. "You did hook up with someone, and you didn't even tell me. Just wait till I talk to you. You're going to get a big piece of my mind."

Feeling immensely relieved, Barbara went downstairs and started to dial Maryann back, but then hesitated, thinking maybe she should wait until Marigold called her before she went down that road. She set the burglar alarm and let herself out of the house. Sure enough, the curtain was pulled aside at the neighbor's, and a face peered out at her. Barbara waved, but the neighbor's face disappeared from the window as she hurriedly dropped the curtains. *Too late to pretend you weren't watching, you nosy old biddy*, she thought. She was in the car driving back home when a niggling thought entered her head. Why was the alarm turned off? She pushed the thought aside. Like Maryann, she was known to be a "wee" bit paranoid at times.

After Barbara got home, she took a shower, swallowed her various meds, grabbed a bite to eat, and imbibed several cups of strong coffee that she made on the fancy coffeemaker her daughter gave her as a Christmas gift last year. She put two days' worth of dishes in the dishwasher. Unlike Goldie, she was not a neat freak. She then sat down in front of the wide-screen TV set and tried to watch an episode of *Law and Order*, all the while listening for her cell phone to ring. At ten o'clock, Marigold still hadn't called. The feeling of relief Barbara had felt after discovering Marigold's missing overnighter began to dissipate, and she started to feel anxious again. The golf banquet was scheduled to start promptly at one o'clock, and the plan was for Goldie to drive over about eleven thirty so that the two of them could ride together. They wanted to get to the banquet facility about twelve thirty, so that they could get a table close to the buffet servers. Maybe then their table wouldn't be the last one called to eat. Maryann hadn't called back either, so that meant Marigold still had not contacted her. The nervousness in Barbara's gut drove her to the bathroom. Anxiety always had a detrimental effect on her digestive system. She carried her cell phone into the bathroom with her and was startled when it rang. She picked it up and answered without looking at the number. "Marigold," she said. "Where are you, you've got me nervous as hell, and your daughter is ready to call out the troops to find you."

"Mom, what are you talking about?" said her son Gregg, who was on the other end of the line. "What about Marigold, has something happened?"

Barbara couldn't keep the disappointment out of her voice as she answered. "Oh, hi, Gregg, I don't know that anything is wrong, but Maryann has been trying to call Goldie, both at home and on her cell since yesterday evening. She called me early this morning, and I went over to Goldie's house. Nothing seemed out of the ordinary, except that the burglar alarm wasn't set, but she wasn't there even though her car was in the driveway. I snooped around a bit and found her overnighter missing, so I figured maybe she hooked up with some guy she met on eHarmony and just decided to maybe, you know, stay over with him last night. Now, I'm getting really worried because she was supposed to come over to my house so we could go together to the golf banquet at the Doubletree. It starts at one o'clock, and I haven't heard from her yet. No calls or text messages."

"Mom, Mom, slow your roll," said Gregg. "You're going a mile a minute. You tend to do that when you're nervous. Now tell me, did Marigold specifically mention to you that she had met a friend and was going out on a date?"

"Well no, she didn't, and that's another reason I'm worried. You know that Marigold and I tell each other everything, and she never mentioned that she had hooked up with anyone. She did tell me she had posted her profile on eHarmony. I just laughed at her, especially since she told me she was looking to find somebody fortyish who wanted to date an older woman. She didn't say 'older' though, she called it 'more experienced.' I called her a 'cougar.' She called me an old-fashioned prude."

"You said she hasn't called, Mom," said my son. "But did you check your e-mail on your computer? Marigold is a techno nut, maybe she sent you a message."

"No, Gregg, I didn't, actually. I hadn't even thought about checking my computer. Marigold hardly ever sends me anything. Hold on while I log on and bring up my e-mail account." Since Barbara hadn't even turned the computer on in the past week, she had to wait for it to power up. She wasn't one of those people who had a love affair with the Internet. She used her computer to play games and write stuff with the word processing program. She checked her e-mail only once or twice a week, and occasionally, she looked something up online or got directions from MapQuest. She signed up for Facebook because Goldie wouldn't leave her alone about it and was surprised that so many of her friends subscribed to it. She rarely logged on herself, and even more rarely made an entry. After what seemed like an eternity, the e-mail page came up. There were about thirty unread messages—none of them from Goldie. Barbara's heart sank even lower.

"Gregg," I said, "I'm looking at my messages now and, no, there's nothing from Goldie. What do you think I should do? What can I do? Maryann is ready to go to the police and file a missing persons report."

"Mom, I can understand how you and Maryann feel right now, but a missing persons report might be a little premature. If Marigold doesn't show up for the golf banquet this afternoon, call me back and I'll start some things in motion. I'll call some contacts at the precincts to make sure nothing about her has been reported, and I'll have someone check admissions to local hospitals in case an accident happened. Try not to get your blood pressure up too much. I love you, Mom, I don't want you stroking out on me."

After getting off the phone with Gregg, she called Maryann back. She answered right away, and Barbara could detect the disappointment in her voice when she realized that it wasn't her mother calling. Barbara told her what her son said about doing some checking if Marigold hadn't shown up by one o'clock. Maryann thanked her and hung up quickly. Barbara know she didn't want to tie up the phone line in case her mother was trying to call.

Barbara really had no heart for getting dressed for a banquet when she didn't know what had happened to her best friend, but she decided to go anyway just in case Goldie showed up there with some excuse for not following their planned agenda. If she did, the excuse had better be an award-winning one, or Barbara was thinking of reading her the Riot Act for scaring her and Maryann so badly. She had trouble concentrating on the drive to the banquet facility and found herself miles over the speed limit on several occasions. She forced herself to slow down. She really didn't need to get a ticket that would send her car insurance premium through the roof. She scanned the parking lot as she drove in. Marigold's Lexus was nowhere to be seen. Once inside, she found a table, put her purse in a seat to save it for her friend and tried to make small talk with the other guests while keeping an eye on the entrance. At one fifteen, when the affair finally got started, Goldie was still a no-show. Barbara excused herself from the table and went into the lady's room to call Gregg. She told him to go ahead with the inquiries he had proposed earlier. Back at the table, she picked at her food until she had to return to the lady's room. Like she had said earlier, anxiety messes with her digestive system.

When the awards were announced, sure enough, Marigold's name was called to receive a trophy. Barbara accepted it on her behalf, hoping with all her heart that she would soon be able to hand it to her best friend. For the third straight year, Barbara didn't win a thing. She loved golf—the game just didn't care that much for her.

On the drive home, Barbara could think of little else but Marigold and how much she meant to her. People who saw them together probably wondered why the two women were such good friends because they seemed to be such opposites. Marigold was, and always had been, outgoing and flamboyant, while Barbara was much more laid-back and introverted. Marigold liked jazz and rhythm and blues and listened to the occasional hip-hop or rap song; Barbara liked country and gospel music. They shared a recently acquired love for the game of golf, but Barbara sucked at it while Marigold played as if she had been golfing all her life. Marigold wore flashy clothes—expensive, flashy designer clothes—while Barbara dressed more conservatively. Not that she could even afford the clothes Marigold bought. Barbara lived comfortably, but she was not wealthy by any means. Goldie, on the other, had money—lots of money—because her deceased husband left her an insurance policy worth a quarter of a million dollars, a portion of which she invested in stocks that kept returning a good dividend. Marigold was very attractive, albeit a little on the heavy side, but her curves looked good, and she had an enviable flat stomach. She typically wore a lot of makeup, but beautifully so, and had a dazzling smile, which she enhanced with those tooth-whitening products. Her hair was always beautiful because she kept a standing appointment at the hair salon every single week without fail. In fact, she really got daring a few weeks back and had blonde streaks put into her dark-brown hair. Barbara pretended to be outraged when, truth be told, she was envious. It looked awesome on Marigold. Barbara was just a tad bit overweight according to the body mass index charts, but most people considered her to be thin. Her few curves were sagging a little with age, especially her butt, and she had never been good at applying makeup. She made do with some lipstick and a little cheek blusher. She considered her best attribute her 38C bustline, which still drew attention from "dirty old men" whenever she was wearing something low-cut. Most people thought of Barbara as merely "nice," but they considered Marigold a little sassy and wicked. That's not to say that she wasn't thought of as a kind person—she was, always willing to help someone in need. She loved her child and her grandchild dearly, although she made Amber call her Nana—she didn't want to called grandmother. She said the title reminded her of someone with gray hair wearing polka-dot dresses and owlish glasses and getting around by using a walker with little wheels on it. Marigold did not have even one visible strand of gray hair. Her hairstylist was paid well to make sure of that. Unlike Barbara, she did not have a problem with arthritis, and she exercised regularly at a gym at least three times a week. She'd probably lose weight and be really svelte if she didn't love rich, fatty foods so much. Also unlike Barbara, she did not suffer from diabetes, but she did have high cholesterol and high blood pressure—mainly because of the way she ate.

When Barbara got home, she pulled into the numbered space provided for her at her apartment complex and noticed that, as usual, she had parked too close to the dividing post. She took the time to ease back out and repark her SUV. A few months ago, she had made the mistake of leaving it parked too close to one of the posts and the next day, backing out in too much of a hurry, she made two big dents in the passenger side door. Her grandchildren laughed for days, telling everyone that "Grandma wrecked her own car without even running into anyone."

Barbara threw her purse and keys on the couch and went directly to her computer to check her e-mail but again was disappointed to see that there were no messages from Marigold. *Where in hell are you, Goldie?* she thought.

CHAPTER

2

At that very moment, hundreds of miles away, Marigold Robbins was wondering the same thing. She had just woken up on a strange bed. She felt groggy and disoriented. The bed was queen sized, and Marigold was tucked in between what felt like silk sheets and covered with a fluffy down comforter. The room was huge, with vaulted ceilings. Heavy drapes were drawn across the windows, but enough light leaked in to let Marigold know that it was daylight outside. She tried to recall how she had gotten here—wherever "here" was, but her mind seemed to be fogged in. When she tried to swing her legs over the edge of the bed, her body felt heavy and wooden. The effort caused her head to swim as if she had vertigo. She stopped and sat still until the room stopped moving and then ever so slowly pushed back the comforter and got her feet on the carpeted floor. When she tried to stand up, she felt nauseous, and the room started to rotate again. Marigold closed her eyes to wait for the world to stabilize. When she opened them again, a man was standing not three feet away from her. She cried out in surprise and apprehension as he started toward her. When he reached her side, he picked her up in his arms and placed her back into the center of the bed and drew the covers back up around her. He smiled down at her and said, "I'm so glad you're awake, my sweet. You just lie quietly for a few minutes. I've ordered you some coffee and a light breakfast. You must be really hungry since you fell asleep before you finished your dinner last night." His voice was soothing, familiar; and inside Marigold's head, memories were starting to emerge.

CHAPTER 3

Barbara was still staring at her e-mail when her phone rang. She rushed to answer it. It was Gregg.

"Mom, I just wanted you to know that I haven't heard anything yet, but you should consider no news to be good news at this point. Marigold's name or description doesn't show up in any precinct reports, and my contacts don't have her or any Jane Doe matching her description in any area hospital. I'm off duty in about an hour, and I'm coming over. We'll get Maryann on the phone, and I'll help you two put together the information needed to file the missing persons report. Don't get upset, but it's been almost twenty-four hours now. It's time."

"Oh, Gregg," she said. "I can't believe this is happening to us. I am so scared."

"I know, Mom," he replied. "But please try to calm down, remain optimistic, and stay focused. That's the best way you can help Marigold right now."

The minute she ended the call, the wave of nostalgia Barbara had been fighting for hours washed over her with an intensity that caused her eyes to tear up. She thought of how much she still missed her husband. One life lesson she had learned was that grief has no statute of limitations, and any reason or no reason at all can bring sad memories rushing back like a strong summer wind. She even thought about her parents who had been gone for years but were still sorely missed. The thought that something might have happened to Marigold to take her out of Barbara's life was way too horrible to even contemplate. She didn't want Gregg to catch her in such a melancholy mood, so she choked back the tears, blew her nose, and washed her face with a cold cloth so he wouldn't see the aftermath of her emotional meltdown.

Barbara had some leftover harvest casserole in the refrigerator, and she threw it in a 350-degree oven along with some heat-and-serve rolls while she waited for Gregg to arrive. She wasn't hungry herself, but she wanted to have something available for him, since he was coming directly over without going home first. One thing she knew for certain about her oldest son was that he didn't miss any meals. That young man loved to eat. She was just taking everything back out of the oven when she heard Gregg first knock then let himself into her apartment. All her children had their own keys. After their father died and Barbara moved into this place alone, she made keys for them and made them all promise that they would always be prepared to check on her. Her greatest fear, irrational as it might be, was that she would die alone in the apartment and no one would even know or find her body for days.

"Hey, Mom," said Gregg as he wrapped his long arms around Barbara in a hug.

"Hey, yourself," she replied. "Thanks for coming over so fast. I don't think I could go through this by myself."

"Sure, you could, Mom," Gregg said with a smile. "You are so much more capable and stronger than you give yourself credit for. What's cooking that smells so good?"

"I figured you might be hungry, so I heated up some harvest casserole, you know the one with chicken, veggies, and lots of cheese. I heated up some rolls too, and there's salad in the fridge. You know where all the dishes are—just help yourself while I get some paper and pens. As soon as you finish eating, I'll call Maryann so we can get started."

"Go ahead and call Maryann now, Mom," said Gregg with a mouthful of casserole. "We can talk while I eat."

The phone rang four times before Maryann picked up. She sounded groggy when she answered. Barbara suspected that she had taken an antianxiety medication to calm her nerves. "Hello, Ms. Barbara," she said. "Please tell me you've heard from Mother, and that she's all right."

"I'm sorry, honey," she replied. "But, no, I haven't had any contact. Gregg is here now and is going to help us put together the information we need for a missing persons report." Barbara heard her quick intake of breath. "Please don't panic, Maryann, Gregg has checked out police reports and area hospitals, and your mother doesn't show up anywhere. That's good news. Intelligent as she is, sometimes your mother is very impulsive. I still believe she'll call us any minute," she lied. "The missing persons report is just a precaution that it's better to get into motion sooner rather than later—just in case."

"Ms. Barbara, I think you know more about my mother than I do," responded Maryann. "But I'll stay on the line and answer whatever questions you have. Let me take some Tylenol first because my head is killing me." Barbara heard tap water running and then Maryann came back on the line. "Okay, I'm ready," she said. Barbara put the phone on speaker so that Gregg could hear anything she said.

"First of all, Mom, we need an exact description of Marigold," said Gregg. "Hair and eye color, skin tone, height, approximate weight, build, and any other specific personal features. Talk to me as you write these things down, so I can get some idea of what you're describing."

"Well," said Barbara, "Marigold currently has brown hair streaked with blonde. Her stylist calls her main hair color champagne. Her hair is cut short. She has dark-brown eyes, unless she has on those hazel contact lenses she wears sometimes. She doesn't have any kind of vision problem, but she says she always wanted to have hazel-colored eyes, so she wears the lenses just for effect. She'll kill me for telling this, but she weighs 170 pounds, and she's exactly five feet seven inches tall."

"That's good, Mom," said Gregg. "Now do you remember if she was wearing those hazel contacts the last time you saw her?"

"No, she wasn't, but I haven't seen her since Wednesday. What about you, Maryann, when did you last see your mother?"

"I talked to her yesterday morning before I went on a job interview, but I haven't seen her since day before yesterday when she rushed by, just for a minute, to pick up her ticket to Amber's dance recital. She just popped in and out, and I don't remember what her eyes looked like. I'm sorry, I don't even remember looking in my mother's eyes, and I may never see her again." She started to wail. "I should have paid more attention."

"Stop it Maryann," said Barbara. "Calm down and just concentrate on getting the proper information down for this report. Blaming yourself for anything at this point is useless."

"Let's get back on track," said Gregg. "Mom, when was the last time you talked to Marigold and knew that she was at home for sure?"

"Well actually, we chatted yesterday morning over coffee. We talked about seeing a movie, but Goldie said she was going to the gym for her exercise around eleven o'clock, and that she'd see me today at the golf banquet. She tried to talk me into going with her, but I haven't been in a gym since I passed out riding the stationary bicycle last winter. I wish I had gone. Maybe I could have …"

"Don't go there, Mom," cautioned Gregg. "First, you don't know that anything has happened to Marigold, secondly, if anything did go down, you don't know that you could have prevented it or just become part of it. Stop speculating. It's much too soon for that. Now, let's get back to the report. I know you can't say for certain what Marigold was wearing yesterday, but you can write down the description of the new purse and the overnighter that you believe she might have taken with her."

"Okay, I'll try to maintain my focus," she said. "The handbag was a large leather Coach, expensive—it cost five hundred dollars, even with Marigold's frequent-customer discount card. It was brown leather but had black and gold straps. Her Gucci overnight luggage is black leather. It's the upright kind with rollers on the bottom and zipper compartments in the front and sides. Marigold's initials are etched onto a brass tag attached to the top zipper. I know exactly what it looks like because she loaned it to me one time when I went to a two-day conference with my business woman's group."

"Mom, what about medications?" asked Gregg. "When you were at her house, did you happen to look in her medicine cabinet to see if she took any meds with her. That may give us a clue as to whether she left voluntarily or not."

"Actually, I didn't open the medicine cabinet. After I found the purse and overnighter missing, I felt better and stopped snooping around. I know Goldie takes all kinds of vitamins and herbs, especially those that supposedly keep you from aging, although I don't even believe there is such a thing. The only real medication she takes is a blood pressure pill. She's meticulous about it, and I don't think she would leave home without it. She's downright anal about her health, except for eating those rich foods." Barbara had almost forgotten that Maryann was listening in on the speaker phone and was startled when she chimed in.

"Ms. Barbara, you forgot about the cholesterol pills. She takes them every night at bedtime."

"Thanks, Maryann, you're right, both of us take the same kind of medication for that. I guess I had a brain burp for a moment."

"Okay, Mom," said Gregg. "Now we need to get together some photos of Marigold, head shots and full-body shots if possible. If you can't find some recent ones here, maybe Maryann can e-mail some to your computer that we can print off."

"I have a ton of pictures right here, all kind of poses. Remember that digital camera you gave me for my last birthday? I take it with me everywhere Marigold and I go. The last few pictures I took are still in the memory—I haven't uploaded them to my computer files yet. Let me run out to the car to get the camera. I took it with me to the banquet thinking I would get a picture of Goldie when she was awarded her golf trophy. I need to bring that in too."

CHAPTER 4

After she drank two large mugs of coffee. The fog in her head lifted, and Marigold remembered the man's name; it was Shelton Maxwell, and they had met at the juice bar in the gym after her workout yesterday—at least she thought it was yesterday. She had seen him there before and had admired him from afar. She had been instantly drawn to him—he was handsome and charismatic, and Marigold was starved for male companionship. After her session at the gym, they drove together in Marigold's Lexus to a nearby Starbucks, where they both consumed huge lattes while they talked about themselves for what seemed like hours. He wanted to know all about her, and Marigold obliged him because he made her feel like she had known him forever. Thinking about it now, she realized that she had probably revealed details of her life that she should not have conveyed to a virtual stranger. At the time, she didn't realize that the things he had revealed about himself were only superficial, generic things. Before long, she felt the stirrings of a sexual longing, even though she was a bit ashamed of the feelings, given the circumstances and the obvious difference in their ages; but she was already smitten. Marigold had always been a passionate creature, and her husband had been dead for a long time. Shelton seemed to feel it too; he picked up her hand, kissed her fingers, and looked deep into her eyes, and said, "Marigold, you are so vivacious and lovely. I feel like I've been waiting for you all my life. You may slap me for saying this, but I want to make sweet love to you." She was mesmerized. He asked Marigold to drive him back to the gym to pick up his car; they exchanged phone numbers and addresses and agreed to meet later for dinner and drinks at a local Italian restaurant. He told her to pack an overnight bag in case he could convince her to spend the night with him. Before he got out of Marigold's car, he pulled her into his arms and kissed her. The heat was incredible. Marigold felt young and desirable again. She was on cloud nine as she drove home, stopping to pick up her dry cleaning on the way.

When Marigold arrived home, she had to rush in to use the bathroom. Her bladder betrayed her like that sometimes. She was anxious to call Barbara to tell her about the gorgeous man she'd just met. Her best friend would probably caution her to go slow, but Marigold didn't care. She was just about to head back out to the car to get her dry cleaning and her laptop when the doorbell chimed at her back door. She was surprised and puzzled when she saw who it was. "Shelton, what in the world are you doing here?" she began, wondering why he was at the back door, but he cut her off by pulling her into his arms for another kiss. Marigold was lost; all common sense went out the window as she gave herself over to the passion she was feeling. He pulled away and said, "Marigold, I couldn't wait until later to see you again. Go pack that bag and let's get out of here and go check into a room at the Hart Plaza. I want to make love to you over and over again without disturbance. Please say yes. I promise to bring you home in the morning." Throwing all caution to the winds, Marigold packed her sexiest lingerie and ran back downstairs where Shelton was waiting. He pulled her into his arms again; she felt a tiny prick in her right arm below her elbow; then she suddenly felt faint, and the room receded and went dark. She didn't remember anything else until she woke up in that silken bed.

Now she was feeling stirrings again, but this time, it was apprehension instead of sexual longing; and instead of feeling young and desirable, she felt like the world's biggest fool. Maxwell looked into her eyes and smiled down at her again; this time, Marigold was chilled instead of mesmerized by that smile. He said, "Sweet, I need you to do something for me. I want to keep you to myself for a long time, and I don't want your family out looking for you, so you need to send them a message to tell them how much fun you're having. You will do that for me now, won't you, sweet. There's a computer right over by the wall, and I'll sit right there with you while you reassure them. I know you wouldn't want them to feel a moment of distress." He handed Marigold a soft robe, helped her into it, and led her over to the computer, his chilling eyes seeming as much of a weapon as a loaded gun. Marigold was mentally kicking herself for being such a fool. No wonder people said there are no fools like old fools. She had been so obsessed lately with finding a man that she had abandoned all good sense and logic. Barbara would be appalled, and Maryann would probably try to have her committed to a mental health institution. *Those might be the least of my worries,* she thought as she sat down at the computer. She had no idea what Shelton wanted with her—it certainly wasn't sex because they hadn't had any, at least that she knew of. Maybe he wanted money. Did he know she had any? She tried to remember the things she had told him while they talked in the juice bar and at Starbucks. Had she mentioned the insurance policy? She couldn't remember for sure. What she did know for sure was that she had gotten herself into some serious trouble here, and she had to come up with a plan to get herself out. No one was coming to get her because no one knew where she was. Hell, she didn't even know herself where she was.

CHAPTER

5

Barbara went out to the car to retrieve her digital camera and Goldie's golf trophy, and when she came back into the house, she heard the tone on her computer that indicated incoming e-mail. She had left the e-mail page open. She was almost afraid to look but cried out in excitement when she did. "Gregg, look, an e-mail is coming through from Marigold. Did you hear that, Maryann, I'll read it aloud for your benefit too? Oh, thank you, God, thank you."

> Hey, Bee-bop, I know you're mad as hell at me for pulling a disappearing act, but I can explain, girlfriend. I met this dee-licious guy—and I do mean dee-licious—he looks just like that actor, Terrance Harris. Beautiful eyes, beautiful body, beautiful everything. Chemistry between us clicked immediately. One thing led to another, and he suggested that we sneak away to a private resort for the weekend. Who could resist? I didn't call you or Maryann because you would have tried to stop me due to both of you being paranoid beyond belief. I am having an absolutely wonderful time. This resort we're staying at is so huge that it's like a scavenger hunt trying to find my way back to our suite. Reminds me of that time in college on spring break when we

forgot our room number and it took us hours to find the right one. I would have called you, but I misplaced my cell, so I'm e-mailing you from one of the many computers in this cavernous place. Anyway, I'll be home in a few days. Call my darling daughter for me and tell her not to worry and not to send out a search party. Oh, Bee-bop, don't forget to water my peace lilies for me.

> Hugs, love, and kisses.
> Goldie

"See, Mom," said Gregg. "Marigold is just having a fling. She's all right. You and Maryann worried for nothing."

"NO," shouted Maryann and Barbara at about the same time.

"There is definitely something wrong. There are things in that e-mail that don't make any sense. Goldie is in trouble, and she's trying to tell us so."

"What do you mean, Mom?" said Gregg, sounding and looking skeptical. "What do you think is wrong with the e-mail message?"

"First, Goldie never, ever, ever, calls me Bee-bop. That was a name that some snooty sorority girls called me in college. Marigold was visiting me at the time, and she confronted them and threatened to kick their butts if they didn't stop calling me that name. Secondly, Marigold and I never went anyplace except home on spring break when we were in college. And that stuff about a scavenger hunt—I don't have a clue what she's talking about. I remember telling Goldie about one scavenger hunt in college at a party. It was in the winter, cold enough to freeze butts off, and kids were running around outside looking for a bunch of useless stuff. I didn't participate, because I thought it was incredibly stupid."

At this point, Maryann chimed in. "And Gregg," she said, "Mother doesn't have any kind of live plants at her house. She has a brown thumb and kills everything she touches. She has a peace lily in the family room, but it's fake—artificial. So, unless Mother has lost her marbles, she's in trouble and is trying to tell us to come find her."

"I don't believe she would have sent me that long e-mail either," Barbara told Gregg. "You know Goldie, yourself, she would have borrowed that guy's cell phone or someone else's to call. She hates impersonal contact. Something's very wrong, and we've got to try to figure out what it is. I can't shake the gut feeling that I've had all day—that my best friend is in danger."

"Mom, I'll admit that if I had read that e-mail without you and Maryann to point out the anomalies, I probably would have taken it at face value. But you know Marigold better than anyone else in the world, so I'll take your word that something is off. I think I need to get someone else at the department involved in this so we can do some serious investigating and figure out how to proceed on this. We don't want to do anything to jeopardize Marigold's situation, whatever it might be."

"Gregg," said Barbara, "is there any way we can find out where that e-mail originated from? They do that sort of thing on *Law and Order* all the time. It's called an IP address, or something like that. If we can find that IP address thing, it might tell us where Marigold is.

"Mom, I don't think it's as simple or straightforward as they make it seem on TV," replied Gregg. "But yes, I can see if I can get somebody in our cybercrimes section to take a look at it. I have to go through channels, though, and I don't know how long it will take. Those guys are real busy over there because of so many Internet predators and identity theft scams these days. It's too late to even try to get something started today, but I'll talk to my commander first thing in the morning."

"Ms. Barbara," said Maryann. "I just thought of something. Mother and I used to play this game with Amber that was called Scavenger Hunt where we had to look at clues and use them to find a place on a big map. Maybe she thought I might remember that."

"Maryann, to tell you the truth, I don't know what to think at this point. I'm so confused about everything that's happened today. I wish I could just start the day over and Marigold would be where she was supposed to be, and you and I wouldn't be wracking our brains, trying to read some sane meaning into a letter that doesn't make any sense. Why would Marigold do this, why would she go off with a total stranger and cause us all this worry? I am so, so extremely ticked off at her that I want to smack her, but if she came through the door right now, I would just hug her instead." Barbara could feel tears of frustration coming on; Gregg must have noticed because he came over and hugged her without saying anything.

"Mom, you and Maryann need to try to get some rest tonight. I know you think you can't sleep, so you need to take a pill or something. I'm taking all this information that we wrote up for the missing persons report with me, as well as a copy of that e-mail. Hopefully you'll hear from Marigold again this evening or tonight—maybe she'll call this time. If she does, call me immediately, I don't care what time it is. If she doesn't, I'm going to get an investigation started first thing in the morning. Whoever gets assigned to the case may need one or both of you to go over to Marigold's house so they can have a look through. If Marigold still hasn't shown up within the next twenty-four hours, all this information will also be entered in the National Crime Information Center Missing Persons Database. We're going to do everything possible to make sure she comes back home safely. Then you can kick her butt if you want too."

Barbara tried her best to smile at Gregg's attempt to bring some levity to the situation but was much too worried to pull it off. She clicked off the phone with Maryann and walked her son to the door. "Thanks for being so good to me, Gregg, and thanks for not thinking I'm just imagining stuff about that e-mail."

"Mom, you always were too hard on yourself. You're pretty sharp, and you have good instincts. If your gut is telling you something is wrong, then I'll take your word for it. I just need to convince my commander that there is some urgency to the situation so he'll put some good people on it. Try not to worry so I hate to see you looking so downhearted."

Barbara decided to take her son's advice. She swallowed one of the prescription sleep aids her doctor had prescribed for her when Herman died. She had only taken them sparingly because she disliked waking up in the morning feeling sluggish. She slept for four hours before waking up for the first time. She usual woke up fifteen or twenty times a night. Her sleep was restless though and filled with strange dreams. The worse dream was about Goldie. Barbara was on the outside of a huge glass maze and Goldie was on the inside trying to find her way out. Every time she thought she had chosen the right path, she would run into a solid wall. They could see other but couldn't hear each other, and they kept reaching out, trying to touch each other through the glass. The most horrible thing about the dream came just before Barbara woke up. She could see a dark, ominous shadow waiting for Goldie around the next turn. She was screaming at Goldie to turn around and go back, but Goldie couldn't hear her. When she woke up from the dream, Barbara's heart was beating too hard. She could hear it echoing in her ears. She wanted to get up right then and make some coffee; instead, she forced herself to lie back down. She was asleep again in a few minutes. When she woke up again, she had forgotten about the scary dream

CHAPTER 6

Somewhere far away from home, Marigold Robbins was also waking up, although regaining consciousness might be a more appropriate term. If she had dreamed anything while she was sleeping, she didn't recall it. The last thing she remembered was Shelton insisting that she drink the pinot grigio he had ordered with dinner. Marigold couldn't believe that she had even been hungry, given the circumstances, but the gourmet squash soup, the Waldorf salad, and the pheasant under glass, followed by an outrageous chocolate cheesecake had been irresistible. It was the kind of food she loved to eat. She supposed that the wine had been drugged because she had slept through the entire night and was not exactly clear-headed right then.

She thought about the events of yesterday. She had interjected some misinformation into the e-mail he had forced (the word he had used was encouraged*) her to send to Barbara. She and Barbara knew each other so well. She hoped her best friend had understood that she was in trouble.* Shelton might know a lot about me, *thought Marigold,* but he can't possibly know about what Barbara and I did or didn't do in college. He can't possibly know what kinds of games I play with my granddaughter. *She hoped that Barbara or Maryann would go over to her house and see that she had left her blood pressure pills behind. They both knew she would never willingly leave home without them. After she had sent the message, Shelton waited outside the bathroom door while she showered and then insisted that she get dressed in one of her own outfits he must have grabbed out of her closet and stuffed into her Gucci* *overnighter.* She remembered that the only thing she had packed was some lingerie. He turned his back while she dressed but did not leave the room. He then led her out of the bedroom, which she now saw was part of a huge suite of rooms. The door to the suite was already open, and they took an elevator up to another floor where a spa was located. Wherever she was, Marigold speculated that the place was huge. The spa was spread out over the entire floor. She counted as least eight rooms as she was led through the building to a luxurious waiting area. Curiously, she did not see another spa patron in the entire place, but then many of the room doors were closed. There was not a single window that she could see. Smiling as though they were a loving couple on vacation, Shelton instructed the spa staff to give Marigold the "royal treatment." She was then given an aromatic cup of herbal tea, which she only pretended to drink and surreptitiously poured into a potted plant when no one was looking. She feared it was drugged like the wine the night before. She was left alone for a time, and she quietly slipped over to the door and tried to open it. She was not surprised that the door was locked from the outside.

When the spa staff finished with the body wrap followed by a total body massage, a facial, a manicure, and a pedicure, and a fresh hairdo, Marigold had almost talked herself into believing that nothing was wrong, that Shelton was just an eccentric rich guy with too much time and money on his hands who wanted to treat her to an unforgettable experience. Her hopes were thoroughly trashed, however, when Shelton led her back to her room, kissed her on the lips, and walked out of the room. Marigold heard the door lock behind him. She ran over to the door, only to discover that there was no way to open it from the inside. The door opened outward, and there were no hinges and no hardware inside. She was a prisoner, pure and simple, and she didn't have a clue as to why. She made up her mind that someway, somehow, she was going to find out. She listened at the door, and when she didn't hear any sound—although footsteps would be hard to detect on that plush carpet—she went over to the window and pulled back the heavy drapes at the window. She was in some kind of complex that had multiple buildings, most of them one or two stories high, reminding her of pictures she had seen of military barracks. She guessed that she was on the fourth or fifth floor, though she couldn't be sure because Shelton had stood in front of the *console on the elevator and blocked her vision of the numbers. There was a huge parking lot but few cars, so she surmised that this was not some kind of a tourist haven. If it was, then business must be bad. In the distance, she could see mountains, so she thought she must be in a rural area. From her vantage point, she couldn't see the road leading in or out of the complex. One of the lower, flatter buildings appeared to have a helicopter pad. She wondered if that was how she was brought here. A sixth sense warned her that Shelton would be coming back soon, so she closed the drapes and got back into bed. She'd take another look later. Sure enough, Shelton unlocked the door and reentered about five minutes later. After dinner with the drugged wine, Marigold had slept through until this morning. Now her fears were returning, and she wondered what else was in store for her today as she heard Shelton unlocking the door to the suite*

CHAPTER 7

Barbara had just finished her morning ritual—diabetes and blood pressure medication, breakfast consisting of oatmeal, low-sugar orange juice, and several cups of coffee—when the doorbell rang. It was Gregg with Maryann in tow. They all hugged and kissed.

"I got in to talk to my commander earlier this morning," said Gregg, "He's not inclined to launch a full-fledge investigation at this point because he said there is no evidence of foul play and that there is no law against an adult disappearing if they want to. He gave me the go-ahead to process the missing persons report, which I did before I left the precinct, and he gave me his okay if I wanted to do some unofficial investigating. I have to keep up with my normal workload, of course. If I can come up with enough facts to convince him that Marigold has been abducted, he'll throw more resources at the case." Barbara's heart fell all the way into her house slippers, and Maryann began to cry.

"Why won't he do that now?" she asked. "Didn't he read that strange e-mail? Why doesn't he believe us? Does he think we're lying or imagining things?"

"Mom, Maryann, please calm down," said Gregg. It's just that he sees so many of these cases where people go off on their own just to get away from families and situations. He's of the opinion that Marigold will show up soon. There's just no real evidence that she was taken. I don't agree with him, but I can understand his position."

"What are we going to do then?" asked Barbara. "I know in my heart that Goldie is in serious trouble, and the authorities are not taking us seriously."

"What am I, Mom?" asked Gregg. "Chopped liver? I am part of what you call the authorities, and I most certainly believe the situation is serious. I've called in a few favors. One of my friends, Rickie Williams, is an ace investigator. He happens to be on furlough right now due to an on-the-job injury. He's coming by in about an hour so we can talk through this thing and decide what to do next. Also, I gave that e-mail to one of the computer guys. He had some top-priority cases to wade through first, but he promised to call me back today, as early as possibly, to tell me what he found out about the origin of that message. We're going to figure this out, Mom, Maryann. You guys have a little faith. We're going to find Marigold and bring her back home."

Barbara realized that she had always been a "glass-half-empty" kind of person. She wanted to believe that everything was going to be all right, but the feeling of dread in her gut persisted. She had recalled that eerie dream she had last night where she and Marigold were trying to reach each other. Try as she might, she could not keep her mind from drifting back to that nightmare scenario. She could see the danger stalking Marigold, but she was helpless to stop it. She didn't believe that she was psychic or anything like that, but she and Marigold always had kind of a sixth sense with each other. One always seemed to know when the other one was in trouble. "I know you two haven't had breakfast," she said. "So, I'm going to fix the works while we wait for that detective to show up. Maryann, please don't tell me all you want is fruit and coffee. I'm not hearing that right now. You need the energy and comfort of homemade waffles, sausage, eggs, and fresh-squeezed orange juice, and I need something to keep me occupied. I won't take no for an answer, so go in the living room and relax while I get busy in the kitchen." Maryann gave a huge sigh, and Gregg threw his hands up in surrender; both of them knew there was no refusing Barbara when she was in her mother hen mode.

Two hours later, at about ten o'clock, Barbara heard the doorbell ring, and opened it to Detective Rickie Williams. His appearance was a surprise. She was expecting a handsome, muscular, *Law and Order* type of guy. Rickie was about five feet eight or nine inches tall, thin, and almost emaciated-looking. He appeared to be in his midforties, and his head was shaved bald. He shook Barbara's and Maryann's hands, and he and Gregg shared one of those comradely man hugs. He declined the offer of food but accepted a cup of coffee.

"Is it okay if I call you guys by your first names?" he asked "I always hate to be so formal."

Barbara assured him that it was fine as long as they could call him Rickie. He said he preferred just Rick. He said he thought Rickie was just a little juvenile for a guy his age with a bald head. Barbara smiled and thought, *I like this guy.*

"Gregg has brought me up to speed on everything that's happened so far. Marigold going missing, Barbara's look-through at the house, the Lexus still in the driveway, the e-mail, but I need to ask a few more questions before we all go on over there and look around more comprehensively. This is no reflection on you, Barbara, but I'm trained to look for things you might not have even thought about."

"No offense taken, Rick. I'm just glad that you agreed to help us find out what could have happened to Goldie. I know you didn't get your training reading mystery books and watching television, at least I hope you didn't." Everybody at the table laughed at Barbara's attempt at a joke.

"Actually, I'm glad Gregg called. This forced vacation I'm on was ordered by my department. I was out investigating a homicide, and I went into an apartment building that had a step caved in, which I didn't see because the hallway lights were punched out. I tripped and fell and sprained my ankle. They considered it an on-the-job injury. I considered it gross stupidity on my part. I told them I was okay to work, but they claimed I was overdue for my stress leave. When you work homicide, they want you to take a week or two off every year to get away from the horror of it all. I've already been fishing and didn't get anything but throwbacks and mosquito bites. I don't bowl, golf, or play tennis. So now, I'm relegated to sitting around the house watching reruns on television. Not my idea of a rousing good time. Now, helping to solve a case—that's my thing. Oh, I'm sorry, I'm rambling. That's enough about me and my motivations. Let me get some information under my belt about Mrs. Robbins." He spotted a framed picture of Barbara and another woman on the end table. The woman could not be described as beautiful, but she was strikingly attractive; she was smiling in the picture—the kind of smile you know is genuine because it reaches the eyes. She had her arm across Barbara's shoulder. He picked up the picture. "Is this Marigold?" he asked.

"Yes, that's Mother," answered Maryann. "She and Ms. Barbara took that picture a few weeks ago when they went on that trip with the church. Mother had just had her hair done up with those blonde streaks."

"She's a very attractive woman. Tell me, Barbara, when you were at Marigold's house, did you check to see if anything was odd or out of place. For instance, if she's on medication, were any of them missing, or could you tell if particular articles of clothing were there or not?"

"No, I didn't open the medicine cabinet, even though Goldie and I have an extremely close relationship, I still feel like some things are an invasion of privacy. I guess I should have though, given the circumstances. And the only things I knew were missing for sure were the new Coach purse she bought on Wednesday and her Gucci overnighter. I just figured that she had probably changed purses and was carrying the new one."

"Don't beat yourself up about it," said Rick. "You couldn't know everything to look for, especially since at that point you didn't even know that Marigold had gone missing. What about her computer, did you notice if it was there?"

"Yes, her desktop was on the computer desk in the family room where it usually is, but she also has a laptop, and I didn't even think to look for that. It's what she uses most of the time. It could be in her car. I'm sorry, but I didn't think to look in the car either."

"Maryann—and this question is for you too, Barbara—has Marigold been acting different lately? I know you might get insulted when I ask this, but could she be on drugs?"

"No, no, absolutely not, Rick," said Barbara. "The only thing that is bad for her that Marigold puts in her mouth is rich food. She does take her doctor-prescribed medicine for blood pressure and cholesterol, but she won't take anything else—not even Tylenol for headaches. She drinks herbal tea when she has a headache. She will drink an occasional glass of white wine, but only one glass at any given time. No hard alcohol at all. When we were much younger, Marigold discovered that she had almost no tolerance for alcohol. Her body doesn't metabolize it well, so she stays away from it."

"She doesn't smoke either," Maryann chimed in. "My grandmother died from lung cancer when I was still a teenager. One time, Mother caught me smoking and she made me eat the cigarettes until I got sick and threw up. Today, they would call that child abuse, but it worked for me. I never put another cigarette in my mouth."

"Here's another thing to consider," said Rick. "Marigold is around the age when Alzheimer's can begin to set in. How is her cognitive health? Any recent signs of forgetfulness, especially things in the short-term?"

"Rick, I'm not exaggerating when I tell you that Goldie's mind is as sharp as a tack," responded Barbara. "She remembers *everything*— even stuff you wish she would forget. She's always doing logic and crossword puzzles and math games. Says that's the way to ward off senility. There was one thing though that Marigold was doing that Maryann and I tried to get her not to. She was signing up for that eHarmony thing on the Internet, trying to meet a man. I know she sent in her profile, but I don't know if she hooked up with anyone. That's what I thought when Maryann first called me—you know, that she might be spending the night with someone. I hope that doesn't shock you, us being in our sixties and all. But I know for sure that she wouldn't stay away this long, and she wouldn't have put those strange things in that e-mail if that's the only thing that was going on."

"Now, you said she was going to the gym on the day she didn't come home," said Rick. "Did either of you talk to anybody over there to see if they saw her there or if they saw her leave with anyone?" Barbara and Maryann shook their heads—no, they hadn't done that.

"What about the neighbor, did either of you speak to her?" asked Rick.

"I talked to her briefly yesterday morning," said Maryann. "She told me that Mother's car was parked in the driveway and had been since she saw her come home around four on Friday, but she said that the porch light hadn't been turned on the night before. Again, something kind of odd. You see, Mother is a bit compulsive. She always turns on the porch light precisely at seven thirty every evening when she's at home. I didn't ask her if she'd seen Mother earlier in the day. I would bet she did though. Mrs. Adams is extremely nosy."

"Okay," said Rick. "One final question before we head over to Marigold's house. Has she ever, to your knowledge, done anything like this in the past—I mean has she ever taken off to be by herself for some reason and showed up a day or so later?"

"Well, I do remember one time," said Barbara. "But it's one of those little things that happened sometimes in marriages. Marigold and her husband had a disagreement. I think he had gone out with the guys and had too much to drink and forgot about their anniversary dinner. Naturally, her feelings got hurt, so she packed her bag and checked into a hotel for two days. She didn't call her husband. Maryann, I don't think you were old enough to remember that incident. Anyway, it convinced him that he should never again take Marigold for granted. But the difference that time was—and remember that we were much younger then—Marigold did call me after a few hours to tell me she was all right. This time though, she didn't call, just made up that excuse about misplacing her cell phone as a reason for sending that e-mail. She never sends me e-mails."

"Now, please correct me if I get anything wrong," said Rick, "but it's my understanding from Gregg that Marigold has a significant amount of money in the bank, something in the neighborhood of four hundred thousand dollars."

"That sounds about right," said Maryann. "I can call the bank and get an exact figure if you need it. I'm a signatory on all of Mother's accounts."

"I think the estimate is good enough for now. This probably won't make any of you feel any better, but I don't get the feeling that

Marigold was kidnapped for money. In those cases, we usually get a ransom demand within the first twenty-four hours, not that there's any hard-and-fast rules. Maryann, you'd better check with the bank, just in case, to see if any money has been withdrawn in the past two days. While you're at it, make a list of credit card numbers if your mother has any. We'll put a trace on them to see if they're being used."

"Of course, she has credit cards," Barbara answered. "Shopping is one of her hobbies. She has an American Express, one Visa Platinum and a Neiman Marcus, and a Macy's store card."

Rick held up on the questions until Maryann got through to the bank. There had been only one transaction on Marigold's accounts since her last social security deposit—a debit card purchase of a purse at the Coach store last Wednesday.

"What about friends and relatives," said Rick. "Have either of you called around to see if anyone has seen Marigold?"

"Well no, actually, we didn't. For most of yesterday, we were hoping she would show up and we didn't want to cause her any embarrassment. I can go ahead and call now, if you think I should, and Maryann can call up the relatives who live nearby. Marigold has a sister who lives in Hong Kong. I don't think we should alarm her just yet."

"I agree with that, Barbara, so why don't you and Maryann go ahead and make those calls while Gregg and I put our heads together to plan our next steps. We should be ready to leave here in about an hour, if that's okay with you guys. Barbara, could I ask you for another cup of that wonderful coffee. I admit that I'm an addict, and caffeine is my drug of choice."

Barbara used the Keurig to make Rick a fresh cup of coffee, then she went into the living room to make her calls while Maryann went into one of the bedrooms to call relatives. As Barbara expected, no one had seen or heard from Marigold in the past two days, and everybody she talked to was shocked and concerned that she had gone missing. They all promised to call immediately if they heard from Goldie. Maryann came out of the bedroom with a downcast look on her face, so Barbara knew her calls had yielded similar results.

CHAPTER 8

In another part of the country, Marigold watched Shelton walk into the room with the usual smile on his face. When she had first met him, she had thought the smile was beautiful and sexy; now, she found it sinister. Just like yesterday, he waited outside the bathroom door while Marigold showered and did the rest of her personal hygiene. He reached in and handed her a soft, fluffy bathrobe to clothe herself in. He wrapped his arms around her and hugged her as he led her over to the bed. Uh-oh, thought Marigold. He wants to have sex with me. I don't know how I can stand it. I could try to fight him off, but who knows what he'd do to me if I did. I'll just have to grin and bear it and hope he puts on a condom. Her fears were unfounded, however. He merely sat her against several fluffed-up pillows and tucked the comforter around her. He then brought over a bed tray just as a waiter knocked on the door to the suite with the food Shelton had ordered. Marigold was disappointed to see that the tray contained only a fruit plate, a milky-appearing liquid, a cup of herbal tea, and an assortment of huge pills. Marigold would have sold her soul for a cup of coffee. She asked him about the pills—what were they, why was he bringing them to her. He told her that they were necessary to "prepare her" for all the good things to come. When she shook her head and refused to take them, he told her that she had no choice; the program would not work without them. "Swallow them down voluntarily, my sweet, with my special beverage, or I will have to force feed them to you. I assure you, that will not be a pleasant experience."

All the while Shelton was talking, he was smiling at her as if they were having the nicest, most normal conversation in the world. Despite the smile, the look in his eyes convinced Marigold that she should do as he said. The pills were so huge that she could only get them down one at a time. The milky liquid had a disgusting, chalky, undertaste, and it was all she could do to keep from retching and hurling the whole concoction onto Shelton's clothes. When she had gotten it all down, Shelton hand-fed her the fruit on the plate just like a lover would. He kissed her on the lips when she was done. "That's my sweet girl," he crooned. "You'll be grateful later, or at least all of womankind will be grateful to you." He laid out an outfit for her, clothing she had never seen before, and told her he would be back shortly. He needed her to send another message to her family. "Just in case," he said. After he left the room, Marigold went into the bathroom and reached her hand down her throat and vomited up everything she had eaten. Maybe the pills hadn't completely gotten into her system yet—at least she hoped they had not. Whatever plans Shelton had for her were not good, she surmised—not good at all. What was this "program" he was talking about and why would womankind be grateful to her?

CHAPTER 9

Marigold's neighbor was peeking again as Rick, Gregg, Barbara, and Maryann pulled into the driveway behind the gold Lexus. Rick took the key from Maryann and opened the car door after donning a pair of latex gloves. If the case ever became official, crime scene investigators would try to get some fingerprints in case the perpetrator had been inside the vehicle. Marigold's laptop, in its carry case, was on the floor in the back of the car. A dry-cleaners bag containing some articles of clothing was lying across the seat. Rick noted that the passenger seat was pushed back farther than the driver's seat. "Barbara, did you ride in this car when you and Marigold went shopping Wednesday?" he asked. Barbara nodded in the affirmative. "How tall are you?"

"I'm only five feet two inches tall," she answered. "And I think I know where you're going with this. The seat is pushed back much farther than it was when I last sat in it."

There was an empty Starbucks coffee container sitting in the passenger-side cup holder. "Did you leave this here?" he asked Barbara.

"No, I didn't. Besides, Goldie would have cleaned it out by now. She is a neatness freak. I can't imagine her leaving trash in here for days. It's just not like her. And she wouldn't leave her dry cleaning in here either."

Rick picked up the cup and placed it inside a plastic baggie. He retrieved the laptop from the back of the car and handed the dry cleaning to Barbara. He then relocked the Lexus, and they all went into Goldie's house. The alarm beeped as the door was opened, and Barbara hurried to punch in the code to silence it.

With Barbara leading the way, they made the tour of Goldie's house; first the downstairs then the basement and garage, saving the upper level for last. Rick did not see anything that he deemed significant, although he was awed at how clean and neat the place was.

Upstairs, Rick first checked the medicine cabinet; all of Marigold's medications were neatly lined up, with all the labels facing out. She had, indeed, left home without them. In the bedroom, he had Barbara and Maryann look through the dresser drawers to see if they tell if anything was missing. Although she couldn't be certain, Barbara thought that several items of lingerie were missing from a drawer that was a bit tumbled as if maybe things had been hurriedly removed; in all the other drawers, all the items were neatly organized and folded. Maryann also thought that several outfits were missing from her mother's closet; she remembered a particularly loud-colored purple running suit that Marigold had recently bought and a beige slack suit that her mother had ordered from a shopping network show just last spring. Rick made a note of everything in a notebook he carried with him. Barbara couldn't but help but notice the look that passed between Rick and her son Gregg. They too were beginning to worry.

Back downstairs, Rick turned on the desktop computer. "Maryann, do you or Barbara know Marigold's password? I'd like to pull up a list of the last sites she might have visited and also get a look at her e-mail. I'm sorry to invade her privacy like this, but at this point, we don't seem to have a choice."

Barbara sat down at the desk and typed in Marigold's password, and together they read the latest e-mails and viewed the list of all the Internet sites Marigold had visited in the last few weeks. Just as Barbara had said, there were a number of visits to eHarmony. As far as they could tell, no one had yet contacted Marigold. They found a visit to a site called Fountain of Youth that neither Barbara nor Maryann knew anything about. When Rick tried to access it, he was asked for the password created for the user. Barbara tried all the passwords that Marigold normally used. Then they tried family birthdays, pets' names, anniversary dates—all the most common passwords people tend to use; none of them worked. Rick said that he would have the computer guys have a go at finding out what Fountain of Youth was all about.

"I believe we've discovered all we can here, guys," said Rick. "Now I need to talk to Mrs. Adams. Given her suspicious nature, I think it best that Gregg and I go over, you know, in an official capacity and all. Barbara, you and Maryann can wait here."

Mrs. Adams looked through the peephole when Rick knocked at her front door. She didn't know him and she didn't recognize Gregg, although he had been at Marigold's house on several occasions. "Who is it?" she yelled through the door. "And what do you want?"

"My name is Rick Williams, Mrs. Adams, I'm a police detective, and the young man with me is Gregg Ross, a friend of your neighbor, Marigold Robbins. Mrs. Robbins has gone missing, and we need to talk to you to see if you might have some information that can help us to find her."

"Go away and leave me alone," she screeched. "I don't talk to strangers, and I don't know anything about my neighbors. I mind my own business." Rick and Gregg almost laughed aloud at that comment; they had both seen Mrs. Adams peering out the window when they pulled into Marigold's driveway.

"Mrs. Adams, Rick and I are going to hold up our identification so that you see it, and then I'm going to insist that you open up the door. We know you're a good citizen and wouldn't want to impede a police investigation." Mrs. Adams opened the door a crack—her security chain was still in place—and peered out at the ID Rick was holding up. After close scrutiny, she took off the chain and said, "Okay, come on in, but I'm very busy, I don't have time to talk to you all day. I told you, I don't know anything. I already told Mrs. Robbins's daughter about the porch light."

"Thanks Mrs. Adams," said Rick. "We already know about that. What I want to ask you is did you see Mrs. Robbins earlier in the day, either when she left in the morning or when she came back in the afternoon? I know you're a good citizen—a member of the neighborhood watch, am I right?"

"I must have been in the shower or something in the morning because I didn't see Marigold leave, but I did see her come back around four o'clock. She was driving too fast and got out of the car and practically ran into the house. People are always in such a hurry these days. She knew I was looking and didn't even bother to wave. Just in too much of a hurry—too much of a hurry."

"Was anyone with her when she came home?" asked Gregg.

"No, she was alone and ran straight in the house, like I said, and when I went over about twenty minutes later to give her a package that came from UPS—I signed for it to keep them from leaving it on her front porch—she didn't even answer the door. I went around to the back to see if maybe she was in the kitchen, but I didn't see her. When I was coming around the house, I thought I heard a car start up in the alley, but that can't be right. Our alleys are closed, no one is supposed to drive in them. I've still got the package if you want to take it to her daughter." She gave them a flat brown-paper-wrapped package. It felt like a book of some sort.

"You've been a tremendous help, Mrs. Adams, and we thank you," said Rick. "And if you happen to remember anything else, please give me a call. I'm leaving you my card with both my cell and home numbers. You should be proud to be such a good citizen and good neighbor."

Gregg chuckled as they headed back across the street to Marigold's house. "Laid it on a little thick at the end there, didn't you, Rick?" he said.

"Yeah, yeah, I know, but I need Mrs. Adams to be an ally. She still might know something important that she doesn't even realize she knows. Remember what our mothers always told us, you can catch more flies with honey than with vinegar."

"Uh-huh," said Gregg. "My mother never told me anything like that. She didn't go around quoting old adages. Said it would make her too much like her own mother." The two men shared a laugh.

"Were you able to find out anything new?" asked Barbara as she opened the door to let Rick and Gregg back into the house.

"Well, Mrs. Adams said she saw Marigold pull into the driveway around four o'clock on the day she went missing. She said that Marigold rushed into the house as if she were in a great hurry. But according to Mrs. Adams, she didn't answer the door about twenty minutes later when she tried to deliver this package to her. And possibly, she heard a car start up in the alley."

"But the alleys around here are closed," protested Barbara. "No one is supposed to drive in them."

"Mom, you know that people do it all the time, mostly to hide and strip down stolen cars. As long as the alley is not physically closed off with a barricade, a concrete barricade at that, people still use them when they want to."

"Maryann," said Rick, "this package is addressed to your mother. It seems to be a book. Would you mind opening it for us?"

When she ripped the paper off the book and read the title, Maryann's face began to color with embarrassment. She handed the book to Rick and said, "I can't believe my mother. Maybe she is suffering some sort of breakdown." It was entitled *The Mature Woman's Guide on How to Seduce a Younger Man*. Barbara put her arms around her godchild. "Don't be too hard on Goldie," she said. "You are too young to realize how lonely for male companionship she's been since your dad died. They did so much together as a couple, and she really misses that. And this thing about younger men, maybe it's her way of trying to put off the inevitable. We all get more afraid of dying as we get older. At your age, the possibility of dying hasn't occurred to you yet. Seeking younger men probably makes her feel more alive—and farther away from the final curtain."

"Mom, I need to get you home. My shift has already started, and I've got to get to the precinct and work on some of the cases I have backlogged. My partner can't cover for me on them all. Rick is going to head over to Marigold's gym to see if he can develop some leads. Maryann, are you staying in town or do you have to get back to see about Amber?"

"No, my babysitter is spending the night. Amber is taken care of, so I'm going back to your mother's house for right now. I threw some clothes into an overnight bag when I drove down here because I was anticipating not making it back home tonight."

The group secured the house, piled into the SUV, and drove away, leaving the gold Lexus sitting like a sentinel in the driveway of what was supposed to be Marigold's safe haven.

CHAPTER

10

Many miles away, Marigold Robbins was sitting in front of a computer. Shelton was standing behind her so that he could see every keystroke she typed as she composed another message to her family. She was wracking her brain trying to think of cryptic ways to warn them of the danger she was in.

> *Hey, Bee-Bop, just checking in. I am having an absolutely unbelievable experience with my Terrance, and I want it to last as long as possible, so I won't be coming home for a few more days. There's a lot more to that gorgeous guy than meets the eye, I tell you. When I get back there, Maryann is probably going to lock me up and throw away the key. You know how prissy she is. She thinks I'm suffering some sort of late-in-life crisis or something. I'm leaving it up to you to make her understand how much I need this. It's like the dream vacation you and I often talked about. Still can't locate my cell phone and, to tell you the truth, I haven't been inclined to go out shopping. Enjoying being pampered, eating in bed, drinking lots of wine, and luxuriating in the heavenly spa treatments I've been receiving. Take care of yourself while I'm gone, Bee-Bop, and make sure you don't stop taking your blood pressure meds*

just because I'm not there to bug you about them. You know how important it is. And tell Maryann to be sure to kiss Rachael for me. She's the only one I miss right now. See you in a few days.

Love, hugs and kisses.
Goldie

When Marigold was finished, Shelton kissed her on the lips and smiled into her eyes. "Now it's time for lunch, my sweet," he crooned. He opened the door to the suite and pulled a waiter's cart into the room. It looked similar to the one this morning, except that raw veggies had been added to the fruit plate. The same pile of huge pills sat along that disgusting-looking liquid, plus a cup of herbal tea that Marigold suspected was drugged. "Eat up, Marigold, there are new adventures in store for you this afternoon. Pills, first, though, and drink down every drop of my special liquid. It's very good for you."

There was no way Marigold could avoid swallowing the collection of huge pills. They were too big to hide under her tongue. She wanted to heave every time she swallowed the foul liquid, but she had the feeling that Shelton would just bring more if she threw it up. As soon as she was finished with the medications, Shelton fed her the fruit and veggies, making sure she ate it all. He sat there until she drank the hot tea; this time, he did not leave the room so that Marigold had no opportunity to try to purge the entire mess. Sure enough, less than twenty minutes later, Marigold was asleep from the drugged tea. Shelton made a call on his cell phone, and two men came into the room with a gurney. "Gently, gently," instructed Shelton, as the men lifted Marigold onto the stretcher and wheeled her from the room. Shelton followed them to the elevator.

CHAPTER 11

Rick Williams's next stop was at the forensic crime lab where a friend of his agreed to see if he could get prints off the Starbucks coffee container he had found in Marigold's Lexus. His friend said that he couldn't get to it immediately, priorities again, but that he would be sure to get it done before the end of the day. Rick then drove over to the Move Your Body fitness center where Marigold was a lifetime member. He showed his credentials to the young lady at the intake desk (her name tag said Bethany) and asked if she knew Marigold Robbins. "Of course," she said. "Everyone here knows Goldie. She's been coming here three times a week for years. A very pleasant, generous woman. She even brings us presents at Christmastime. Why do you want to know, has something happened to her?"

"Well, we're not sure Bethany," said Rick. "But her family hasn't seen or heard from her since early Friday. I understand that she was in here on Friday?"

"Yes, she was, for her usual workout. She was here for two hours like she always is."

"I see this is a co-ed facility," said Rick. "Did you see Mrs. Robbins leave perhaps with a man on Friday?"

"I didn't actually see her leave," said Bethany. "But I did see her sitting at the juice bar with one of our guest patrons. He'd been here a few times, said he was contemplating becoming a member, but he never actually signed up."

Rick was disappointed. "So, he didn't fill out any information card, or anything like that?"

"No, he brought in one of those certificates good for seven free visits. You can get them in pizza places, video stores, and online. We figure that a certain percentage of people who take advantage of the free visits will actually sign up for a membership."

"Bethany, you wouldn't happen to remember his name, would you? asked Rick.

"Let me see, I think it was Shelby or Sheldon or something like that. But I didn't catch his last name. He never did get much of a workout when he was here though, he was always chatting up the women—the older women especially. Seemed like quite a charmer, actually."

"Can you describe him for me?" asked Rick.

"Well, he was a light-skinned African-American, and I pegged him as midforties, although you know some people are older than they look, about six feet tall, slender, but muscular build, beautiful eyes, sort of hazel-colored maybe. You know, he sort of reminded me of that actor, you know, the one who played that hustler—oh, what's his name? Oh yeah, now I remember. It was Terrance Harris. That's who he reminded me of. He always wore designer workout clothes. I had the gut feeling that he had money and always wondered why he was here for free visits instead of in a private club somewhere. Go figure. He was really handsome. I can see how the older women would fawn over him. He wasn't my type, though," said Bethany. "I was leaving once at the same time he was getting into his car. It was a late-model silver BMW. I don't know exactly what year though. I'm not that good with cars."

"You've been a big help, Bethany," said Rick, "I'm going to leave you my card. Call me if you remember anything else. By the way, the person that's running the juice bar, was she on duty on Friday morning?"

"Yes, her name is Carla, and actually she runs the juice bar full-time. She's not one of the fitness trainers. Couldn't pass the test to get certified. Detective Rick, you take one of my cards in case you decide to join up. You look like you need to buff up a bit, and I'll get a commission if you sign up with me. Got to earn my keep, you know," Bethany said with a smile as she handed Rick the card.

Rick put the card in his pocket. He believed in physical exercise; in fact, he ran five miles a day, rain or shine, summer or winter, but he wasn't into pumping iron and the machine stuff they offered in fitness clubs. He believed guys who had to have huge muscles and six-pack abs had low self-esteem and used their bodies to make themselves feel good about something.

Rick stopped at the juice bar and ordered a fruit-and-veggie smoothie to drink while he talked to Carla. She said she remembered Goldie sitting at the juice bar on Friday talking to a tall, handsome African-American man.

"Do you happen to know the man's name?" asked Rick.

"No, but I've seen him in here a few times. Now, don't get me wrong, I'm not nosy or anything like that. I mean I don't listen in on people's conversations on purpose, but I just happened to hear what they were saying. They made a date to meet at Starbucks for coffee. I remember thinking that Mrs. Robbins was going to negate the effects of the special health drink I had just made for her by putting caffeine in her system. As a matter of fact, she seemed so taken by that guy that she didn't even finish her drink. I had to pour it out. What a waste of good fruits and veggies. We buy them fresh every day from the farmer's market next door, you know. It wasn't my business, but I could have told her that the guy was full of crap and just shining her on because he was always hovering around the older women. Mrs. Robbins was the first one I saw leave out with him though."

Rick thanked Carla for the information and gave her a tip after he finished his drink, which was surprisingly good for something supposedly "healthy." He went back over to Bethany and asked if any of the women she had seen "Shelby or Sheldon" talking to were in the club right now. Bethany said she couldn't be sure, but she might have seen him chatting up Mrs. Wilson, who was currently sweating on a treadmill over in one corner of the gym. Rick wandered over and identified himself and asked the woman if he could speak to her for a minute. She nodded but pointed at the timer on the machine, indicating that he would have to wait until her workout was finished. Rick nodded and stepped aside. After another ten minutes, the machine started to slow down and finally stopped. Mrs. Wilson stepped off, wiped the moisture from her face, and took a big swig of water from a water bottle hanging around her waist. She appeared to be in her sixties, with salt-and-pepper hair.

"What is you want to ask me, young man?" Mrs. Wilson began with a smile. "I paid the speeding ticket, and I've been good ever since."

Rick smiled back. "No, it's not about anything you've done, Mrs. Wilson, but I'm glad that you have seen the error of your ways, so I won't have to get out my handcuffs. On a serious note, do you happen to know Marigold Robbins? She's one of the regular patrons here."

"Why, yes, I do, we do our floor exercises and aerobics together every Monday. Why are you asking? Did something happen to her?"

"Her family hasn't heard from her since early Friday, and they've filed a missing persons report. I'm trying to track her movements after her daughter's last conversation with her."

Mrs. Wilson was shocked. "Oh my God," she exclaimed. "Do you think she's been kidnapped? And her being such a nice lady and all."

"Before she left here on Friday, she was seen talking to a tall, light-skinned African-American man, around forty years old, stylishly dressed, who apparently has been in here on several occasions. Bethany thought she might have seen this man talking to you."

"If it's the guy I think you're talking about, yes, we did have a conversation, but he seemed to lose interest when he found out I was happily married. He was handsome and charismatic, beautiful eyes—some of the women commented that they wouldn't mind hanging around him. Me, even if I wasn't married, I don't fathom dating men who seem young enough to be my son. Besides, there was something about him that I didn't like. He was always smiling, but there was something in his eyes that said the smile was a lie, if you know what I mean."

"Do you happen to remember what the conversation was about, and did this guy tell you his name?" asked Rick.

"He said his name was Shelton, although I don't remember him ever giving me a last name, and the conversation was mostly small talk, but he did ask me if I would mind telling him my age, said he had developed some antiaging stuff that would make me even more youthful looking than I am. Said he had a process that could turn back the clock. What BS. Nobody can reverse nature. Everybody gets old, and when you get old, the only thing that happens from there is you get older—you don't go backward. Maybe he thought I had money or something and that fountain of youth thing was just a ploy to get his hooks into me. Or maybe it meant absolutely nothing, and I'm just as paranoid as my children think I am. Anyway, I didn't tell him my age, told him that a lady never, ever reveals her age and that a gentleman never asks. I'll tell you though, young man, because you're too polite to ask. I'll be sixty-seven on my next birthday."

"Fountain of youth," said Rick. "Is that your terminology, or was it his when he was talking about this so-called process?"

Mrs. Wilson thought for a minute. "To tell you the truth, young man, I don't remember for sure. It just popped into my head just now. He might have said it, but I might have just been thinking from the things he said that what he was trying to do was come up with a fountain of youth. I sure hope that nothing has happened to Goldie and that you find her soon. Her daughter must be frantic. Her best friend Barbara too. Goldie talked about her all the time, said they were more like sisters than friends."

"Thank you for speaking to me, Mrs. Wilson," said Rick. "And Shelton wasn't lying to you. You look very young. I would've pegged you for no more than forty-five."

Mrs. Wilson's smile broadened. "You tell a convincing lie, young man, but I know better. The ruts in my face are big enough to puncture a tire, and I've got much more salt than pepper in my hair. Thank you for the lie though, it was sweet. I'll tell my husband. Maybe it'll make him a little jealous, and he'll pay a little more attention to me."

Rick determined that he had probably gotten all the information at this location that he was going to. His phone signaled an incoming text message. It was Gregg; one of the computer technicians wanted to talk about what he had found in Marigold's e-mail. Rick sent a text saying that he would be at the station in thirty minutes.

CHAPTER 12

Back at Barbara's house, Maryann got on her cell phone and called the babysitter to check on her daughter while Barbara went into the kitchen to peruse the refrigerator to see what she could cook up for lunch. Maryann needed to eat to keep up her strength; Barbara needed to eat because she was diabetic. Neither one of them heard the computer beep to signal incoming e-mail. When Barbara thought to check, she yelled out excitedly, "Maryann, it's your mother, she's sending another message." Maryann and Barbara exchanged looks as they read the new message, which had been received fifteen minutes prior. It was the same as the previous one; some things contained in the message didn't make sense. Barbara sent a text message to Gregg. She avoided calling him on his cell when he was on duty. Gregg sent a reply. saying that he needed to clear some paperwork but that he and Rick would be over in about an hour to scrutinize the latest message.

Harold, the computer technician, told Rick and Gregg that he had checked out the e-mail from Marigold. "I'm having trouble tracing the IP address because it was cloned many times. The nearest I can get to an origin is a general geographical location. It came from somewhere in Missouri, in the mountains in the general vicinity of that theater place—Branson. I'll keep trying, but I don't think I'm going to be able to narrow it down much more. Too bad, the woman didn't call or send a picture using a smart phone. You know they have a GPS system that provides for automatic embedding of geographical information, it's known as *geotagging*, in pictures taken with the phone. The pictures are also time stamped. A lot of people don't realize that they're giving out their home addresses to the world when they post pictures from their phone on the Internet. They could avoid publishing sensitive information by using what's known as a metadata removal tool for photos before publishing them on the Internet. Dangerous business, but the public just isn't as educated as they should be about that kind of thing.

"The other thing you asked me to check on, 'the fountain of youth,' I got 2,250,000 hits. Many of them were about the legendary spring that Juan Ponce de León was supposedly searching for when he discovered Florida, a few were for health spas, several sites were for cosmetic surgery centers—there was even one was for a resort campground for kids. The clear majority of them though were for sites that talked about antiaging products or processes. The site Marigold visited talked about revealing an 'ancient secret' to reverse the aging process. I logged on to the site, and it directed me to another page where I was directed to answer a questionnaire. Based on the answers, it said I would be directed to another site for more specific information. I think the site a person is directed to depends on the information filled in on the questionnaire. Without knowing what Marigold filled in on her questionnaire, I don't know specifically what she looked at once she left the generic site. Apparently, once she filled in her information, she deleted it from the hard drive. The information is still out there somewhere in cyberspace, and I may be able to recover it, but I need more time. I also tried to identify the owner of the website but have run into some privacy issues that I don't think I can get past without warrants, and based on what you've told me so far, you don't have a basis for warrants right now. I'm not giving up though, I still have a few tricks up my sleeve. Any luck at coming up with her password?" he asked. "That's our best bet for quickly getting more information on this website."

"No luck so far," said Gregg. "But we'll keep trying, and we appreciate that you will too. I know you're doing me a favor on top of your official workload. I owe you a six-pack, my man."

Harold laughed. "Yeah, and remember I drink real beer, none of that lite stuff. That's for girls."

Gregg thanked Harold for his efforts, and he and Rick headed to Barbara's house. On the way over, Rick brought Gregg up to date on the information he had garnered at Move Your Body, and Gregg told Rick about the latest e-mail that had come in from Goldie. They both agreed that the longer Marigold was missing, the less the likelihood that she would come home safely. They were also almost certain that this was not a typical kidnapping for profit given there had still not been any ransom demand. They agreed not to share these thoughts with Barbara and Maryann just yet.

Barbara had printed out copies of the latest e-mail and waited patiently while Gregg and Rick both read the contents. Then they discussed what Barbara described as the scavenger hunt clues. "Just like in the first message," said Barbara, "Goldie is calling me Bee-bop, and she talks about Maryann locking her up and throwing away the key. I think she's trying to tell us that she's locked up somewhere. When we were younger, before our children were born, Goldie and I used to talk about going on a dream vacation with our husbands. We had always wanted to visit the Pacific Northwest, and we said that we'd like fancy hotel rooms with a view of the snow-capped mountains. Of course, those were just pipe dreams. At that time, we were struggling with our careers and trying to make ends meet. Once the children came, and we were better off financially, we just never got around to taking the trip. And another thing in the message is off. Goldie would never eat in bed. She's too anal about cleanliness. She'd worry that she'd drop crumbs in her sheets or something. Rick, I know you might think some of these things I'm mentioning don't mean anything, but remember that I've known her all my life. Some habits just don't change."

"You're right," agreed Maryann. "Mother never let us eat anyplace except at the dining room table. We couldn't even have popcorn in front of the television."

"I agree that the 'dream vacation' reference is also a definite clue," Rick said, "because Harold from the computer crimes lab said the first e-mail originated from somewhere in a mountainous area in the state of Missouri. Marigold is one smart lady."

"She also told me in the letter not to forget to take my meds," continued Barbara. "I think that's her way of warning us that she can't take her own meds because she doesn't have them with her."

"The last thing she said is definitely a clue that something is not right" said Maryann. "She told me to kiss Rachael for her. Rachael is her sister who lives in Hong Kong. We haven't even seen her in about three years."

Rick agreed with the women that Marigold was definitely sending them clues, but nothing so far was leading them any closer to finding out where she was and for what purpose. He shared with them the information he had found out at the health club. "Marigold was right on in describing the guy as Terrance Harris. One of the women I interviewed said that exact same thing. I believe his first name is Sheldon or Shelton, but no one recalled him ever mentioning a last name. So, we at least have a general description of the guy. It's also interesting that Mrs. Wilson mentioned 'fountain of youth.' That's the name of the website Marigold recently visited. Mrs. Wilson said she couldn't recall if this 'Terrance-looking guy' said those words of if the terms came out of her own head."

Gregg's cell phone rang just then, and he indicated that it was a call from the station. "I'm sorry, Mom, Maryann, but I've got a problem with one of my cases. I've got to get back to work, but I'll be back as soon as my shift is over. While I'm at the station, I'll run what we've learned by the commander. Maybe he'll relent and give us some more resources to help find Marigold." He didn't add the words he was thinking: *before it's too late.* "Rick, what about you?"

"I'm headed over to the Starbucks located near the health club to see if anyone remembers Marigold and the guy she was with. Maybe somebody heard something that might help us out. I'll keep everybody posted on whatever I learn. Meanwhile, ladies, keep the faith. We are making some progress, and that's encouraging."

CHAPTER

13

Somewhere else, Marigold was waking up—again. She had a slight headache—like the aftermath of drinking more than one glass of red wine. She was alone in the huge bed; she could see from the light peeking from around the drapes that it was daylight, but she couldn't be sure it was even the same day. The last thing she remembered was drinking the drugged tea. There was a small ache at the side of her head behind her right ear, and when she reached to touch the spot, she found a small round bandage and wondered what had happened. Had she been injected with something? Suddenly, she started to remember a weird scenario. A dream, maybe. She was lying on a stretcher in a room that seemed to be a hospital operating room. A figure in a mask and gown leaned over her. She couldn't tell if it was a man or a woman. She couldn't open her eyes, couldn't speak, but she could hear the gowned person keeping up a conversation with someone else in the room. Someone out of sight. The voice of the figure leaning over her was slightly muffled, perhaps because of the mask. The figure standing over her was saying, "This one is different from the others. They were all indigent, homeless throwaways that no one cared about. She has a family, and someone is likely to come looking for her. I didn't sign on to this to spend the rest of my life in jail for kidnapping." Marigold couldn't understand the reply from the figure who was out of sight, but the voice sounded agitated. The masked person continued to speak, "Yes, yes, I understand that you needed a healthy specimen, but I'm not sure this one is as healthy as you seem to think she is. Her blood pressure is much higher than the protocol calls for. Are you sure she's not hypertensive? Of course, I have medications that can stabilize her blood pressure, but how introducing them into her system will affect the procedure is anybody's guess. This is a mistake, I tell you. She's not ready yet. She's only had two doses of the prep. Her system needs to be purged of toxins before we inject the formula into her body. Remember what happened the other times. We need to wait." She couldn't make out the words of the reply, only that the words were angry, threatening. The gowned and masked figure continued to protest. "Yes, I know you're anxious to get on with the trial, but what good would it do for her to stroke out on us?" The angry voice of the person out of sight (Marigold suddenly realized that it sounded like Shelton) grew even more agitated. Finally, the gowned and masked figure said "All right, all right, I'll go ahead with it. It will be your responsibility if she ends up like the others." She could hear what seemed like the buzz of a bee flying around the room, and she was frightened. She had a phobia about flying things, especially bees.

She felt the bee settle on her head right behind her ear; she tried to cry out as she felt the intense pain of a sting.

Marigold's hand strayed again to the small bandage behind her ear and realized that maybe she hadn't been dreaming after all. She started to shake with fear, but then she made herself focus on her family and her home, and the shaking stopped. Since she was alone, she again eased herself out of bed. The vertigo stopped after a minute or so, and Marigold went over to the window and pulled back the drapes. She tried as hard as she could to get a different vantage point than she had when she looked out before. There was a ledge directly below the window, and Marigold wondered, briefly, whether it was possible to climb out the window and down to the ground without breaking her neck. But she didn't see any way to get from the ledge to the ground. Besides, where would she go if she could get to the ground? In one corner of the complex, she spotted a paved road that seemed to be leading up toward the mountains. The parking lot was sparsely populated, just as before (she counted eleven vehicles), but she saw a woman walking toward a black SUV. Marigold pulled away from the window just as the woman looked up toward her room. Marigold hoped the woman hadn't seen her; if so, there would probably be consequences. She rearranged the drapes and got back into bed and, despite her resolve not to, her eyes grew heavy, and she fell back to sleep.

CHAPTER 14

When Gregg got back to the station, he went directly to his commander's office. He brought the man up to date on the investigation into Marigold's disappearance, and he showed him the latest e-mail received that morning. The commander was still not convinced that anything sinister was going on. The things that seemed "wrong" with the e-mail was just speculation, he said. There was not any hard evidence that Marigold was involuntarily missing. He gave the okay for Gregg to continue on his own to investigate but, again, declined to assign other police personnel to the case. Gregg was disappointed, to say the least, and a little more than pissed off, but he held his tongue. He really wanted to know how his commander would be acting if his own mother was missing under similar circumstances.

Meanwhile, Rick was interviewing staff at the Starbucks a few blocks from the Move Your Body health spa. He had talked to some of the employees who said they did not remember Marigold. "Man, do you know how many people come in here every day?" one of the male employees, one Randy Watkins, said. "It's all I can do to remember how to make the specialty coffees they order. I don't think I even look at their faces."

He finally talked to one young lady, Constance, said her name tag, who did remember Marigold; at least she remembered Marigold's companion because he was so handsome, looked just like that actor, Terrance Harris, she said. Bingo, thought Rick.

"I was thinking to myself," said Constance, "when they ordered their coffees, whether she was his mother, given the apparent differences in their ages and all. But when they sat down over there to drink their coffees, he reached across the table and took her hand and raised it up to his lips and kissed it. I knew then what was up. Younger guy, older woman—she was probably one of those cougars. I couldn't understand what his problem was though, him being so handsome and all. Maybe he was one of those freaky guys with an Oedipus complex—you know, a guy that wanted sex from somebody that reminded him of his mother."

"Well, I don't know if I agree with what you just said, Constance, I really just need to know if you happened to hear what they were talking about. Maybe they talked about their plans for the rest of the day."

"We're much too busy around here to be able to concentrate on one or two customers," said Constance. "So, no, I didn't hear what they were talking about. They sat at that table in the corner, the one farthest from the counter, and talked for about forty-five minutes, or so. I kept waiting for them to leave. We only have a few tables in here, and we're not used to people tying one up for so long, especially once they're done with their drinks. The guy saw me looking over at them after about thirty minutes, and he came over and ordered another latte. He took it with him when he left; they got into a gold Lexus. He had his arm around her waist, and she was looking up at him like he was the sun shining, or something."

"Constance, do you remember if they paid by cash or credit card?" asked Rick.

"He used cash," she answered, and Rick was disappointed again. He was hoping for a last name for Shelton.

Rick thanked Constance for the information, bought himself a grande mocha with a caramel shot, and gave her a one-dollar tip, which she thanked him for. He looked over his notes and went over the facts he had so garnered so far. Marigold had apparently met this guy, Shelton—last name unknown—who supposedly looks like the actor Terrance Harris, at the Move Your Body health club. According to witnesses, the two had talked briefly at the juice bar in the health club and then they had gotten into Marigold's Lexus and driven together to the Starbucks a few blocks away for coffee and more conversation. They had been seen getting into Marigold's Lexus after they left the coffee house, so it was probably safe to assume that Marigold drove him back to Move Your Body to pick up his own car, which was possibly a silver BMW, model year unknown. Marigold had then driven home, stopping on the way to pick up her dry cleaning, and according to the nosy neighbor, rushed into the house in a hurry. She had left her dry cleaning and her laptop in the vehicle. Maybe she had made a date with this Shelton and wanted to make sure everything inside the house was in order, maybe she was excited, or maybe she just had to pee, Rick didn't know, but there was a reason she was in such a hurry. He went over the timing in his mind and estimated that Marigold had arrived home somewhere near four o'clock. Her daughter had tried to call her at five o'clock and didn't get any answer; so, Marigold must have gone missing somewhere between four and five. Whoever took her, and Rick's money was on this Shelton character, had to have a vehicle of some sort because he didn't take Marigold's Lexus. This theory was consistent with Mrs. Adams's story of hearing a vehicle in the alley behind Marigold's house. It was also a fact that no ransom demands had been made, there had been no activity on Marigold's bank accounts or credit cards, so Rick was reasonably sure that the abduction—and he was positive now that it was an abduction—was not about money. He speculated, although he didn't have any facts to back it up, that the whole thing was tied up with this mysterious "fountain of youth." He would bet the farm on it. Whoever had taken Marigold was trying to buy time by having her sending "well-being" messages to her family. Why? Maybe, the guy wasn't all that secure that they had disappeared without a trace; maybe he needed more time to cover his tracks completely. Otherwise, why bother sending the messages? He didn't want the authorities involved, so he had something to hide. Something in his past, maybe, that he didn't want dug up that might possibly lead to his whereabouts. Rick felt like he had before him a one-thousand-piece jigsaw puzzle. He had found all the edge pieces but had yet to begin to fill in the inside. He had to find out who this Shelton was. His gut feeling was that Marigold Robbins's life depended on it.

CHAPTER 15

When Marigold awoke again, Shelton was sitting on her bed, smiling down at her, and gently stroking her hair. When she cringed, and tried to pull away from him, he said "No, no, my sweet, you wouldn't want to hurt my feelings now, would you. Two days ago, you were oh so willing to let me make love to you. You wanted me to caress your body and lie naked next to you. Now you're afraid of me? That just won't do. I promise to take very good care of you. After all, you are my golden egg—you are going to make me very rich and famous, after which I plan to retire to a private island somewhere very far away from here and live in luxury all the rest of my days. My life's work will have been accomplished. You would never have guessed when we met, my dear, that your future held such promise, would you." *He sounds certifiable,* thought Marigold. Just then, there was a knock at the door to the suite; Shelton opened it, and through the bedroom door, Marigold could see a white-coated waiter come in with a covered tray. Shelton took the tray and shut the door behind him. "Here's your dinner, my dear," he said and uncovered the tray to reveal the same disgusting combination of fruits, veggies, pills, milky liquid, and tea. She fought back tears. She'd be forced to consume everything, she'd fall asleep after drinking the drugged tea, and then Shelton would be free to whatever he wanted to with her, take whatever liberties he wanted, and she wouldn't even know. She thought about the dream that probably wasn't a dream—that masked and gowned person in the operating room. And that talk about her fate being to make Shelton rich and famous. What were they doing to her? She was growing more afraid by the minute. Sure *enough, he made her down the pills with the chalky liquid then watched as she ate the fruit and veggies. Suddenly defiant, Marigold decided to put a crimp in his plans, even if only temporarily. When she started to sip the tea, she deliberately inhaled so that some of the liquid would go down the wrong way. As expected, she choked and started to cough, and just like she had planned, she coughed so hard that everything she had consumed spewed up in a stream of vomit. Shelton jumped out of the way and shouted, "You imbecile, now you've ruined the prep for today. I can't continue the procedure until tomorrow because I don't have another dose ready. If you ever do this again, you will be very, very sorry." He got up angrily and pushed the serving tray out of the room. "You can go hungry tonight. I refuse to bring you anything else to eat and see how you like staying in this disgusting bed until morning. I will not send anyone in to clean it until then." As soon as he slammed out of the suite, Marigold ran over to the computer. This time, she was going to send a real message; she turned the computer on—nothing happened. She sat down and cried tears of frustration. She should have known; the computer had been disabled. She was grateful for one thing; if she slept tonight, it wouldn't be because she was drugged. Shelton had been so angry about her throwing up that he had forgotten that she hadn't finished drinking the drugged tea. Marigold wet a towel in the bathroom and cleaned the vomit from the comforter. It was left with a slight pungent odor that was tolerable. Fortunately, none of the mess had gotten on the bedsheets. Marigold crawled between the sheets and pulled the covers up to her chin. She closed her eyes and tried to think of a way out of there. She thought about the wait staff that brought the trays to her suite. Maybe they didn't know she was being held against her will. Maybe she could find a way to signal them that she needed help.*

CHAPTER 16

After leaving Starbucks, Rick made a call to his friend at the state crime lab. He wanted to know if they got any hits on the fingerprints from the abandoned coffee container he had found in Marigold's car. "We did get a hit," his friend said. "But it's a print from a cold case crime scene. We can't identify the person it belongs to."

"Tell me about the case," said Rick.

"Well, about two years ago, a homeless woman, around sixty-five years of age—they never knew for sure because she was never identified—was found dead under a freeway bypass in Chicago. The medical examiner ruled it a homicide because there was evidence of serious blunt force trauma to the head, which could have caused death. She said 'could have' because there was also evidence of some kind of toxic substance in the woman's body. The medical examiner could not rule out that substance as causing or contributing to death because she was never able to identify what it was, so the official cause of death was listed as 'indeterminate.' She did say that the stuff showed up as a luminosity in the brain when they scanned it. The fingerprint was lifted from a plastic tag around the woman's wrist—you know like the ID bracelets they put on you at hospitals. This one had some numbers on it, nothing else, and they couldn't find out where it came from. Since the cause of death was not actually ruled homicide, not a lot of time and effort was put into it. The case was never solved, and the body was never claimed. It was buried in the local Potter's field. Sorry, I couldn't ID the print for you."

"Nothing comes easy in this line of work," said Rick. "I really appreciate your help. Do me another favor, when you get the chance. See if you can pull up any other cases of elderly women found dead where the medical examiner may have found a similar strange substance in the brain. I hope you can't find any because I don't like the implications of that, but any lead is a good lead right now."

"I don't know if what you're asking is even possible, given the number of cases nationwide where the cause of death may be questionable, but I'll give it a shot. I don't think there's a national database that correlates such information. I can't tell you when I will be able to get back to you, though, Rick. We're real busy here trying to solve open cases where we know for sure that we're looking at homicide."

The news Rick had heard from the forensics lab about the fingerprint match wasn't something he was ready to share with Goldie's family and friends just yet. If that guy Shelton, or whatever his name might really be, had been involved in a homicide, then he was indeed very, very dangerous. They needed to find Marigold fast, or they might be finding her body somewhere. The only problem was that Rick didn't have a clue as to where to go from here.

CHAPTER

17

It was just a little after six o'clock, and Barbara and Maryann had just finished dinner when Maryann's phone rang. It was Mrs. Adams, Marigold's neighbor.

"Hello, Maryann, has your mother come home yet?" she asked. When Maryann indicated that she had not, Mrs. Adams said she had some new information that had just come to her attention.

"What is it, Mrs. Adams?" said Maryann.

"Well, you know we have a neighborhood watch meeting over here once a month. We had the meeting earlier today. It was my turn to be hostess, you know, I had to cook a meal and everything. I cooked up a special casserole that everybody said was absolutely scrumptious, and I also served homemade pound cake with straw—"

"Mrs. Adams, please," interrupted Maryann. "What did you find out that concerns finding my mother?"

"Oh, I'm sorry, my dear, I do tend to go on sometimes. One of my neighbors who lives right down the block from Marigold's house heard that same car in the alley that I told that nice young detective about. Only she was out in her backyard pulling up weeds from her flower garden, you have to keep up with them you know, or they'll overrun everything. Well, anyway, Flossie had just stood up from weeding and she got out her phone—she has one of these smart phone thingies that take pictures and everything—to take a picture of her roses to send to her sister in Seattle—when this black van drove past her in the alley. Well, Flossie figured whoever was driving was up to no good because the alley is closed and nobody is supposed to be back there, so she leaned over and quick snapped a picture of the car to try to get the license plate number to give to the police. She says the picture's kind of fuzzy, she can't make out the numbers, but she saved it anyway. She watches those crime shows where they can use computers to enhance stuff so they can read it. Will you tell that nice, young man to come by and talk to Flossie? She'll be glad to have some company."

Maryann thanked Mrs. Adams and hung up. She told Barbara what the woman has said, and Barbara sent a text message to Gregg and Rick, asking them to get in touch as soon as possible. Rick called ten minutes later and said that he would head right over to the neighbor's house to talk to her. Barbara suggested he stop in at Mrs. Adams's first so she could let Flossie know he was on his way. After all, Flossie had never seen Rick before, and older people were notoriously suspicious of letting strangers into their houses, especially in the evening hours.

Rick rang Mrs. Adams's doorbell and saw her peeking out of the window before she opened the door. He explained that he needed her help again and asked if she would mind calling her neighbor, Flossie, to let her know he was coming.

"I'll do better than that," she said as she pulled on a sweater and retrieved her house keys. "I'll walk down there with you."

Flossie opened the door immediately when Rick walked up on her porch; she must have been watching out the window because she didn't even wait for the doorbell to ring.

"Good evening, Bell," she said. "And I suppose this is the nice, young detective you told me about. How are you, ah, Mister—sorry I forgot, what did Bell say your name was?"

"I'm Rick Williams, ma'am, you can just call me Rick, and I hope you'll allow me to call you Flossie. I have an aunt with that same name, and you remind me of her."

Flossie invited them in. She had a pot of tea and a plate of cookies sitting on her dining room table. "Sit down, both of you, and have some tea and cookies, they're homemade, fresh out of the oven."

Rick didn't want cookies, but he wanted to have Flossie trust him so that he could get the best information he could from her, so he sat down and helped himself to one of the chocolate chip cookies. It was actually quite good, and he reached for another one. Flossie poured tea and offered lemon and sugar, which Rick declined. If he had to drink tea, he preferred it straight.

"Flossie, now tell me exactly what you saw in the alley Friday afternoon." he said.

"Well, I was out weeding my flower gardens. They're the best on this block, you know," she beamed. "I was done with the front and side yards and was just finishing up with the back on the side of my garage out by the alley fence. I keep my phone in my pocket whenever I'm outside, just in case somebody calls, so I decided it was a good time to take a picture of my roses to send to my sister. She's always bragging about her flowers. I'm sure her gardens are not as spectacular as mine. Anyway, I heard a car engine just as I stood up, and I remembered that time last year when a stolen car was ditched in the alley and got stripped down before the police even got here. I'm the president of the neighborhood watch, you know, so I decided it was my responsibility to try to take a picture and notify the police, just in case, you know. That alley has been closed for two years. Nobody in this neighborhood uses it, and nobody is supposed to be back there. One of our neighbors, Henry Woodson, is lazy and trifling, and he recently threw a big pile of junk into the alley. The neighborhood watch is reporting him to the city. It would serve him right if he gets a ticket and has to go to court for littering. Anyway, the van—I believe it was dark blue or black, the driver had to slow down to get past that trash. That gave me a chance to snap a picture of the license plate. When I looked at it, I couldn't really make out the numbers, but I watch those crime scene investigation shows on television. They can always figure out the numbers. I uploaded the picture to my computer—wonderful things those computers—and printed you out a copy." She handed him a fuzzy-looking photo that showed the back of a dark-colored minivan. Flossie was right, the license plate numbers were indistinct.

"Flossie, did you get a good look at the driver as the car went by?" asked Rick.

"Well, no, can't say I did, because I was trying to stay a little bit out of sight. But I know the driver was a man, and I get the impression that there was another man in the passenger seat."

"Another man, are you sure?" asked Rick. "You didn't see Marigold Robbins in the vehicle at all?"

"No, I didn't, if Marigold was in there, she was lying down out of sight."

Rick used his cell phone to call Harold, the computer guy, to ask him if he could do anything with a fuzzy smart phone photo of a vehicle license plate. Harold instructed Rick to send the picture to his computer and said he would see what he could do. "Flossie, did you save the photo on your phone?" asked Rick. Flossie nodded in the affirmative and brought up the photo and handed her phone to Rick, who in turn, transmitted the photo to Harold's computer.

"Thanks to both of you, ladies, for being such good citizens," he said as he grabbed one more of the chocolate chip cookies. "I'll be sure to let you know if this leads us anywhere in our investigation. It just may be a significant break."

The two ladies beamed as they saw him to the door. He heard Bell Adams say as she closed the door. "Flossie, your flowers are not the best in this block, mine are. My yard could make the cover of *House and Gardens* magazine."

Uh-oh, thought Rick, *I'm glad I'm out of there. I wouldn't want to get in between two senior citizens bickering over their flower gardens.* A guy in that position could get seriously hurt.

Rick called Gregg and relayed to him the information he had gleaned from the neighbor Flossie and explained that Harold, the computer techie, was trying to enhance the photo she had pulled off her cell phone so that possibly they could identify the license plate of the vehicle he believed had been used to carry Marigold away from her home. "If we can identify the vehicle," he said, "we can issue a BOLO for it." He also told Gregg about the cold case that had been brought to his attention but cautioned him not to share that with Barbara and Maryann just yet. Gregg agreed that such information would panic the two women even further, but at the same time he realized that the latent print off the Starbucks coffee container being a match to a print from the scene of a homicide of a woman in Marigold's age range was compelling and disturbing news.

CHAPTER 18

Marigold could no longer see daylight leaking from around the drapery, so she concluded that night had fallen. She couldn't tell exactly what time it was; there were no clocks in the room. She got out of bed, pulled back the drapes, and looked out at the moonlit night. It made her think of a line from the poem "The Night before Christmas" that her mother used to read to her when she was a child, the part that said, "Not a creature was stirring, not even a mouse." She wandered around the room, pulling open closet doors and dresser drawers, trying to find something that she could use to help herself. The dresser drawers contained only the lingerie items she had foolishly thrown into her bag when she thought she was leaving for a romantic encounter with a lover. There was not even a pen or pencil or even a piece of paper in the dresser or nightstand. I am certainly not in a hotel room, *she thought after seeing the empty drawers.* Because there is no Gideon Bible. *The closet contained three outfits, in different colors, all in her size, but she didn't recognize any of them. They were too plain for her tastes. Shelton must have bought them and put them there himself. Her empty Gucci overnighter was on the floor, and her new Coach bag was on the shelf, and she pulled it down and looked inside. Her wallet with all her credit cards were inside, intact, as well as her car keys and the keys to her house. Her cell phone was missing. She opened her wallet and took out the latest picture she had of her granddaughter, Amber. She looked at the ticket to the child's dance recital she had picked up from Maryann on Thursday and wondered if she would ever get the chance to see her granddaughter dance. Goldie rechecked the bathroom; she had been in there several times but thought that maybe she had missed something. She found items of personal hygiene: shower gel, toothpaste, mouthwash, deodorant, and her makeup kit sitting open on the vanity. Nothing else. She opened the medicine cabinet. It was empty, and it made her think of her medications that had been left behind. Her blood pressure was probably very high at this point.*

Goldie suddenly realized that there was nothing impulsive or spontaneous about Shelton bringing her here. It must have all been carefully planned, which also meant that the encounter in the juice bar at Move Your Body had not been accidental. It was all orchestrated. How long had Shelton—if that was even his real name—been watching her and contemplating making his move? She tried to think back to when she had first seen him in the health club. She couldn't recall exactly, but it seemed to her that he first came in about three weeks ago, always charming, always talking to one or the other of the ladies who did their workouts at the same time that she did. It occurred to her, now, looking back, that he had been like a politician working the room. She was nothing more than a stupid, vulnerable old lady who had been duped because she had too high an opinion of herself. She could almost hear Barbara saying, "Goldie, this never would have happened if you had been facing reality and acting your age." Suddenly, the lyrics of a song from the 1980s popped into her head as she thought about how she had allowed a total stranger to seduce her the way Shelton did. She had gone way beyond anything she had ever even contemplated before. The lyrics struck a chord with her now. They said, "Don't go chasing waterfalls. Please stick to the rivers and the lakes that you're used to.'" Had she stuck to a mode of behavior that she had adhered to all her adult life, she wouldn't be in this predicament right now. If Melvin hadn't died ... but no, she thought. There's no use in my going there. None of us have control over life and death, but we can control our own behavior, and I know that—I have a PhD in psychology, for God's sake. That's where I failed miserably. *If there was a heaven, and if Melvin was looking down at her right now, he would know that she had failed him too; her sexual yearnings now felt like a betrayal to the love they had shared for over forty years.*

Goldie thought a lot about the entry door to the suite, which had no latch or knob on the inside. She wondered how Shelton got in and out.

Either he had some kind of remote device, or there was a sensor inside the suite which could be activated to unlock and open the door, sort of like the plates on the walls at hospitals that you had to press. It occurred to her that Shelton was always out of her direct line of sight when he opened the doors for the waiters to bring in the trays. She checked the walls, feeling all around the molding, but found nothing. She walked a grid across the carpet in front of the door, thinking maybe there was a plate under the carpet. She found nothing. Discouraged, she went back into the bedroom and lay down on the bed. It still smelled slightly of vomit. Despite all the stress and fear she was feeling, and once again, despite her resolve not to, Marigold Robbins fell asleep.

CHAPTER 19

Many miles away, after Gregg had come and gone, Barbara had also fallen asleep. Maryann had decided to go home after all to make sure her daughter was all right. The babysitter said that Amber had become unusually anxious; the child had always been very intuitive, and she seemed to feel that something was wrong, and she kept asking about her mother and her Nana. "I'll be back first thing in the morning," she said as she left the house.

Barbara slept restlessly; she had declined to take a sleeping aid because she knew the darn things could easily become habit-forming. She kept waking up, and each time she did, she remembered that she had been dreaming about Marigold. Sometimes they were in familiar places doing familiar things; sometimes the dream took on an ominous note—once, she and Marigold were running and someone was chasing after them. When they were children, Barbara had always been the faster sprinter and, in the dream, she outran Marigold. When she looked back, the figure chasing them had caught up with her friend. She screamed, and when Barbara ran back to try to help, Goldie and her captor disappeared from sight. Barbara was left standing alone on the sidewalk. She didn't seriously believe in psychic phenomena, so she concluded that the dream was just a manifestation of the anxiety she was feeling for Goldie.

Rick Williams didn't get much sleep at all. When he got home, he heated and ate a microwave dinner, his standard bachelor's meal, and fixed himself a stiff drink. He spent some time going over his notes of witness interviews, trying to see if there was anything significant that he might have failed to ask. He spent a lot more time on his computer, looking at different sites for "fountain of youth" on the off chance that something might hit a chord with him. So far, Marigold's website visit and the as-yet unidentified vehicle seen in the alley were his only leads (tenuous as they were) to this Shelton guy, last name unknown. There had been no activity on her bank accounts or credit cards. There had been no ransom demands. No one had seen her or heard her voice since Friday. The only proof of life were those odd-sounding e-mails supposedly sent by Marigold. Rick finally gave up about midnight and tried to get some much-needed shuteye. He knew the clock was ticking. Tomorrow was Monday. Marigold had been missing since around four, four-thirty on Friday. In Rick's experience, this did not bode well.

True to her word, Maryann returned to Barbara's house early the next morning. Her eyes were puffy and red-rimmed. It was obvious that she had been crying—probably a good part of the night. Gregg joined them for breakfast before heading in to the station for his shift. After he left, Maryann and Barbara decided to go to church to pray for Goldie's safe return home. There was always a prayer service held on Monday mornings. Barbara was a staunch believer in the power of prayer; Maryann, not so much, but she didn't quite "disbelieve" either. Praying certainly couldn't hurt. At the sanctuary, they ran into a few mutual friends who joined them at the altar in a prayer of intercession on behalf of Marigold. They stayed for the remainder of the service then returned to Barbara's house to wait for news from Rick or Gregg, or possibly another message from Goldie.

CHAPTER 20

Marigold had slept fitfully on and off throughout the night and woke up feeling both hungry and thirsty. Shelton had made good on his threat; he hadn't returned to the room last night, nor had he sent anyone in to clean it. She got out of the bed and went into the bathroom and drank several cups of water from the sink. She had a foul taste in her mouth and had just finished brushing her teeth and rinsing with mouthwash when she heard the door to the suite open. She stiffened, expecting to see her captor; instead, a woman wearing the white smock of a health care professional entered the suite, pushing a cart in front of her. Marigold wondered if it was the same woman she had seen out of the window (was it yesterday?), walking toward the black SUV on the parking lot. She began to speak to Marigold in a calm, cajoling voice, like she was speaking to a small child. "How are we this morning, my dear, I'll bet we're hungry, aren't we? Dr. Marshall told me that you regurgitated your meal last evening, so he wanted me to come in especially early this morning to get some nourishment into you before your treatment today. I've brought you some fresh fruit, a poached egg, some whole wheat toast infused with flax seeds, a glass of fresh-squeezed orange juice, and some herbal tea. Doesn't that sound good? Dr. Marshall will bring in your medications a little later."

"I don't know any Dr. Marshall, and who are you?" asked Marigold. "Why is Shelton keeping me here against my will. He kidnapped me, you know, right out of my own home. When the police catch you with him, you're going to jail too 'cause you're helping him keep me prisoner. If you help me get out of here, I'll tell the police that you did and maybe they

won't arrest you. Please help me. My family must be frantic. They don't know where I am."

"Now, now, my dear, you must try to remain calm. You see, agitation is not good for someone in your medical situation. And of course, your family knows you're here, my dear, because by law, they would have signed the papers to commit you. And you're lucky, too, my dear, this is a very exclusive institution. Only the very privileged are admitted here for treatment of their problems. Here you not only get the best medical treatment, but you also experience all the amenities of a luxury resort. Be assured that we will do everything we can to get you feeling better so that you can go home. But you must cooperate and allow us to do that."

"What in heaven's name are you talking about?" Marigold practically screamed. "Are you saying that this is a mental hospital and you think that my family put me here because they believe I'm crazy? No, no, that's wrong, absolutely wrong! Shelton lied to you, do you hear me, he lied to you. He made me send my family e-mails to trick them into thinking that I'm on a fabulous vacation trip. He kidnapped me, I don't know why—I don't know if it was for money or what, but he did kidnap me right out of my own home, and he's keeping me drugged. See that cup of tea on that tray, it's drugged, and if you don't believe me, drink it yourself and see what happens to you. Please believe me, help me get out of here, or at least get me a cell phone so I can call for help. Shelton is doing something bad to me, I can feel it. He even took me to an operating room and made a bee sting me behind my ear." Marigold pulled her hair back. "Look, can't you see the scab?"

Marigold was so desperate to get the woman to understand her plight that she didn't realize that she sounded just like what the woman had been led to believe she was—a paranoid schizophrenic.

"You see what happens, my dear, when you allow yourself to get so agitated, you start to imagine all sorts of things. Like I said, it's my job to get some nourishment into you, so please sit back down and eat the breakfast that's been prepared for you. Here, I'll take a few sips of the tea so that you can be assured that it is not drugged."

Marigold suddenly realized that the woman was not a part of Shelton's scheme, whatever it was. The horrible thought settled in that she really was being held in a nuthouse for the wealthy. This woman, *whoever she was, had been duped into believing she was just another crazy patient.* This means, *thought Marigold, that my situation is even worse than I thought. I'll never get anyone who works here to believe me because they all think I'm a raving lunatic.* So, she decided she had to "go along to get along," so to speak. She had to bide her time until she could come up with a plan. She just had to hope and pray that her time wouldn't come to an abrupt end before she could do it. "Okay, okay," she said. "I'll eat my breakfast," which she proceeded to do, even drinking the tea, though she still feared it was drugged. When she was done, the woman patted her hand like she was comforting a small child and pushed the tray cart ahead of her to the door of the suite. Marigold walked behind her to the door of the bedroom, thinking that maybe when the woman opened the door she could overpower her and get out of the room. But then what? Marigold had no idea where she was or how she would get away from this place in the mountains. She could get lost and die from exposure or starve to death. No, she needed to wait until she had more information. She tried to see how the door was unlocked, but the woman's body was blocking her view. But she did hear the little click that released the lock and caused to door to open. A man clad in blue scrubs—an orderly, she supposed—was standing in the hallway. It was a good thing that Marigold had not tried to rush the woman. She should have known that there was someone there to back her up.

After the woman left, Marigold waited for the drugged tea to take effect, and when nothing happened, she realized that the woman had been telling the truth. It was just herbal tea. Shelton was probably saving the drugs for later—for her treatment, whatever that meant. Marigold went into the bathroom, took a shower, put on her robe and sat down in the easy chair by the bedside to await the inevitable. She tried to remember some of the mental exercises she used to keep her mind focused; without a clock or television, she was having a little trouble keeping track of what day it was. She thought it was Monday but couldn't be sure because the drugs Shelton had been giving her had a disorienting effect. Like Maryann, Marigold was not devoutly religious; she didn't subscribe to any particular religious beliefs, but she did believe that a higher power than man exists in the universe. Marigold closed her eyes and began to pray to whatever being that might be listening.

CHAPTER 21

Rick woke up around seven o'clock on Monday. He realized that he had missed something in his investigation and was mentally kicking himself for his "brain burp." It had occurred to him, just as he was waking up, that either the health club or the Starbucks might have a video surveillance camera. If either one did, they might just have a tape showing the face of the suspect. Rick picked up his cell phone and punched in the numbers for the Move Your Body health club. He got a recorded message saying that the club hours were from eight o'clock until five o'clock. When he tried the Starbucks, he was surprised to find out that the coffee shop had been open since 5:00 a.m. Rick went into the kitchen and got some coffee started while he showered and shaved and dressed. He perused the morning newspaper while he ate a bagel slathered with cream cheese and drank three mugs of strong coffee. Then he headed out the door. His first stop was Starbucks. "Is Constance working today?" he asked the young man at the counter. His name tag said his name was Nate, and his title read Shift Manager.

"Nah, Connie doesn't work on Sundays and Mondays," said Nate. "Says she can't miss going to church on Sundays, and they like to schedule off days two in a row, so they don't put her on the schedule for Monday either. She has enough seniority to get away with that. Not that I mind because Sundays are a lot slower than other days. Today, we're going to get a whole slew of people in here trying to get some adrenaline going before they get to work. What can I get for you, man?"

"Actually, I wasn't looking for coffee, Nate. My name is Rick Williams, and I'm a police detective. I'm investigating the disappearance of a woman who was seen in here on Friday in the company of a man who may have abducted her. Connie remembered the woman and the man in here. She was very helpful, but now I have a few more questions."

"Well, I wasn't here on Friday," said Nate. "Thursdays and Fridays are my regular days off, so I won't be of any help to you."

"Maybe you can," said Rick. "Is that a video surveillance camera that I see mounted just above the door outside your shop?"

"Yeah, it is," said Nate. "And we've got one inside too. It's just disguised. See that flower pot up there with the sunflower in the middle? That sunflower is the lens."

"Where do you store the videotapes? Do you have the ones from Friday still in the store?"

"You're out of luck on that, man," said Nate. "These cameras don't use video tapes. They use digital video recorders—modern technology, you know. The information is transmitted from here to our security company and they store it on computers. I can give you the name of the security company." He pulled a card out of a file box next to the cash register. "Here you go." He handed Rick a card with the name and phone numbers for an outfit called Sentinel Security Professionals.

Rick thanked Nate for this information and ordered a tall caramel mocha, complete with whipped cream, even though he really didn't need it because he had already consumed quite a bit of caffeine before leaving home. He was already beginning to feel like he was wired.

He went out to his car, and while he sipped his mocha, he used his cell phone to call the number on the card Nate had given him. Someone answered on the first ring. "Sentinel Security, David speaking, how may I help you?" Rick identified himself and explained what he was looking for. He stressed the urgency of the situation.

"Well, here's the thing," said David. "Those are private files belonging to the Starbucks Company, and I'm not authorized to give you access unless I have written permission from someone at their corporate offices. If you can give them a call and have them fax me a standard release form, then I can let you see what we have."

"David," implored Rick, "did you not pick up on the fact that I said a woman's life may be in danger? I really need to get a look at what was recorded in that Starbucks store on Friday. It may give us a good photo of our suspect."

"I did understand you, Detective," said David. "But maybe you didn't understand me. I have a wife and three children at home that I have to put bread on the table for, and I am not about to do anything to put my paycheck in jeopardy. Sorry, but I really can't help you until I get official authorization." He read off the number to the corporate office then said, "You'll have to excuse me, I've got another call coming in."

"Damn," said Rick as the call disconnected. "What a jerk. Marigold, it looks like we just can't catch a break for you." He called the number David had given him and got a similar idiot on the phone who told him he couldn't have permission without a subpoena. Rick hung up in disgust. He'd deal with that issue later.

The next stop on his agenda was an encore visit to Move Your Body health club. He didn't see any of the staff he had interviewed the day before. He went through the same explanation he had at Starbucks and was told by the young lady at the counter that she knew they had cameras but didn't know anything about how they worked or where information was stored. She said the club manager didn't start work until 1:00 p.m., and that he could come back later.

"Look, Sandy," he said, reading from the woman's name tag. "This is critically important. Do you have your manager's home phone number—you know in case of emergencies?" When Sandy nodded in the affirmative, Rick said, "Well, this is an emergency. Call her right now."

Sandy retrieved the manager's number from a Rolodex behind the desk and reluctantly keyed in the number. "Mrs. Preston, I am so sorry to bother you at home, but—no, ma'am, there's nothing wrong at the club, it's just that there's a policeman here who says he needs to see footage from the surveillance cameras from Friday. Yes, ma'am, I told him, but he says it can't wait until you come in. He said it's about that woman, Marigold Robbins, who went missing on Friday. Yes, ma'am, I'll tell him. Good-bye." Sandy ended the call. "Mrs. Preston said the video equipment is locked up in the back, and she's sending someone over that knows how to work it, if you can just wait about an hour."

"I'll wait in the car," said Rick. He finished sipping his coffee and got Gregg on the phone and brought him up to date. About forty-five minutes later, he saw Bethany, the girl he had talked to before, drive up. When she spotted him, she motioned for him to roll his window down. "Hey, Detective Rick," she said. "My manager told me to get my hocks over here and help you with the video stuff. So, let's get to it. I'm not getting paid overtime for this, and I've got other, better things to do on my off day than hang around this place."

"You don't know how much I appreciate this, Bethany," said Rick.

"Well, why don't you show me your appreciation by signing up to be a member of the club," she said with a smile. "I get a commission for every member I sign up, and business has been lousy lately."

"How about I treat you to lunch sometime instead," said Rick. "I hate working out more that I hate castor oil. I'll buy whatever you like and deliver it right to you at work any day you want. Do you like Chinese?"

"Well, if that's the best you can do, I guess I'll have to accept," said Bethany, as she led him to a locked storeroom in the rear of the building and punched in a code at a console to open the door.

She went over and used a remote control to turn on the video equipment and used the rewind function to get back to Friday morning's footage. Rick had her press play, and he watched until finally he saw what he was looking for. A silver BMW pulled into the parking lot and a tall, light-skinned African-American man emerged. He seemed aware of the camera and kept his face down or averted so that Rick never could see his face in totality. At one point, there was a pretty good profile shot. The guy actually did look somewhat like that actor. The crime lab people might be able to do something with it. Later, Marigold and the man emerged from the health club and climbed into Goldie's Lexus and drove away. Again, the camera caught a good profile view of the man sitting in the passenger seat. Rick felt like he had struck gold when they returned in the Lexus and the man got out and climbed into the BMW. As he pulled out of his parking space, the camera got an image of the license plate full on. "Bingo," said Rick. "We finally caught a break." He called Harold, and the computer guy talked him through the procedure for sending the entire video recording to his computer. Rick then called Gregg at the station and read him the license plate from the silver BMW and told him to get started on checking various Department of Motor Vehicles databases to see if they could match the owner with the car. "I'll be in to help you out," said Rick. "But you'll need to clear it with your commander first because I'm still officially on furlough."

When Rick got to the station, Gregg had already located the information on the BMW. The vehicle was registered to a Travis Mitchell, age fifty-nine, with an address in a high-rise apartment downtown. The Department of Motor Vehicles photo looked nothing like the guy shown on the video tape. For one thing, he definitely was not African-American.

"I used the reverse directory to get a phone number," said Gregg. "But when I dialed it, I got a message saying the phone was disconnected. I've already contacted the phone company to see if we can get phone records for that number. They might insist on a court order though before they give us the information. Look, Rick, I've got to drop some files off at the courthouse. What say you after that, we take a little detour and ride downtown to check this guy out?"

Forty-five minutes later, they arrived at an apartment building that was modern and upscale, ten stories tall. Rick and Gregg had to use a console in the front vestibule to ring the security office; a burly security guard whose name tag said "Joe Daniels, Chief of Security" first looked them over then asked them to hold up their identifications so he could see it. Only then did he buzz them in.

"I apologize for the scrutiny, but you can't be too careful these days," he said. "Burglaries are up all over the city. People in this building pay good money for us to protect their property."

"Joe, we're here investigating the disappearance of a woman named Marigold Robbins. She was seen with a guy driving a silver BMW. According to the Motor Vehicles Records, the car is registered to a guy named Travis Mitchell. Do you happen to know the guy?"

"Yeah, as a matter of fact, I do," said Joe. "I mean I don't know him personally, but I know who he is. He's that guy that moved out in the middle of the night— didn't even try to get his security deposit back. He must be flush if he could afford to give up two thousand dollars—that's what tenants have to plunk down as security in this place. We wouldn't have known he was gone, but he left the keys and a note in the apartment saying that he had to leave suddenly because of an emergency. He left an address for a post office box somewhere in another state—I believe it was Minnesota or Missouri ... anyway, I remember it started with an *M*—to forward his mail to. The cleaning service that cleans the apartments once a week found the note. Funny thing though, I never saw him driving a BMW. Maybe he kept it at his girlfriend's or something. He was always driving a black SUV, maybe 2008 or 2009 model year, had a parking space assigned to him in the garage."

"You mentioned a girlfriend, Joe," said Rick. "You ever see him with a female companion?"

"Nope, I was just guessing when I said that. I don't know if he had a girlfriend or not, I just figured if he owned a BMW, maybe that's what he did with it."

"Do you know if he was friends with anyone else who lives here in the building; ever see him talking to another tenant?"

"Not that I recall," said Joe. "But so many people come and go that I can't keep track of any particular one in my mind. But wait, I saw him in conversation with one of our maintenance men several times. Maybe he had problems in his apartment, I don't know."

"Do you know his name and where I can find him?" asked Rick.

"His name was Charlie, something or other, I didn't know his last name, but the building manager might."

"When did Travis Mitchell move out?" asked Gregg.

"If I remember right, it was about two weeks back, but you can check with the building manager, he would know for sure. His office is right down the hall, first door on the right. I just saw him go in there. You came at just the right time because he's in and out all day—he manages more than one apartment building."

Rick and Gregg went down the hall and knocked on the glass door. They could see a man sitting behind a huge desk. The label on the door read, "Charles Paulson, Manager." The manager looked up and beckoned them inside.

"Mr. Paulson, I'm Rick Williams and this is Gregg Ross. We're investigating the disappearance of a woman by the name of Marigold Robbins. She was seen on Friday in the company of a man who we believe abducted her for reasons yet unknown. That man was driving a vehicle that is registered to one of your tenants—or should I say ex-tenant, because your security chief told us that Travis Mitchell moved out about three weeks ago, leaving you in the bag for a month's rent. Is all this information accurate?"

"Yeah, that's right," said Paulson. "And I've got to tell you that I was totally taken by surprise. The guy was here for about two years, always paid his rent on time. I inspected the apartment after I learned that he had vacated. There weren't any damages or anything. We had to keep part of his security deposit because of the rent, but he didn't even try to get the rest back. He must have been in a hell of a hurry to go somewhere."

"You said the apartment was in good shape, so let me ask you this: were you aware of any maintenance problems the guy might have had? Joe Daniels seemed to remember him talking with a maintenance man named Charlie on more than one occasion."

"I've got a log here of maintenance problems dating back for about a year. Let me take a look." Mr. Paulson scanned several pages of a loose-leaf binder that he pulled off one of the many bookshelves that flanked his desk. "Let me find the right entries. I'm old-school, not that good with computers. Here we go. No, I don't see any maintenance issues for that apartment for the past year. So, I wouldn't know why he was talking to Charlie. Maybe they were just shooting the breeze."

"We're going to need to talk to Charlie," said Gregg. "Is he on duty right now?"

Again, Mr. Paulson pulled a binder from a bookshelf. "Here's the schedule for this week. Uh, no, Charles Evans is on two consecutive off days." He pulled out a pad. "I'll write down his address and phone number for you." He handed the slip of paper to Gregg. Gregg immediately pulled out his cell phone and dialed the number written on the paper; he got a message saying that "Charlie can't take your call now, call back later."

"Mr. Paulson, did Travis Mitchell leave anything behind—any personal belongings, clothing papers, things like that?" asked Rick.

"No, the place was clean except for the furniture. We rent the units already furnished, you know. I don't know why security didn't notice that he was vacating. He must have had to carry boxes and stuff down to his car, probably made more than one trip to the garage, unless he had been planning on leaving for a while and took stuff out piecemeal, maybe in his briefcase or something."

"We need to get a look at his lease application and any other paperwork you have that this guy filled out when he rented the place."

"Sure, sure, I'll cooperate any way I can," said Paulson. He went over to a file cabinet and rummaged through it until he came up with a slim file folder with Travis Mitchell's name on the tab. "Here's everything I have on the guy." He went over to a copy machine in one corner of the room and copied everything in the file; he then handed over the original to Rick. "You don't need to bring it back. I made a copy for our records."

"Mr. Paulson," said Rick, "now I know that you aren't necessarily privy to your tenants' comings and goings, but do you remember seeing Travis Mitchell with a woman, or any visitors for that matter?"

"To tell you the truth, Detective, I probably can't identify 95 percent of the tenants by sight, so I can't honestly say I know visitors from tenants. They keep me so busy running between buildings, and when I'm here, I'm stuck back here in this office. No, I wouldn't have noticed any of Mr. Travis's visitors. Sorry about that."

"Well, it was worth a try," said Rick. "And thank you very much for your cooperation, Mr. Paulson. If you think of anything else about Travis Mitchell, anything at all, even something you might think is not worth mentioning, please give one of us a call. We're both leaving you our cards with contact information on it."

When they got in the car, Gregg tried Charlie Evans's phone number again; it went to voice mail just as it had earlier. Since the man lived an hour away, Rick and Gregg decided they wouldn't make a trip to his home unless they could get in touch with him first. They didn't have any time to waste. Rick was driving, so Gregg read through the files Mr. Paulson had copied for them.

"Mitchell's apartment lease application is pretty sketchy. He doesn't list anybody's name under 'personal references,' but he does list his employment history. According to this, at the time he signed the lease, he was working for an outfit called New Generations, with an address in New York City, but he listed a local hotel as a past residence. When we get back to the station, I'll start an Internet search to try to find what this 'New Generations company' is all about. Maybe, it'll lead us to Travis, and if we find Travis, he might lead us to Shelton and Marigold."

"I'm anxious to see what Harold came up with on the license plate for that vehicle that Flossie saw in the alley," said Rick. "It's the same kind of vehicle that Joe Daniels said Travis Mitchell parked in his parking space in the garage. Meanwhile, let's put out a BOLO on that BMW."

CHAPTER 22

Shelton came into Marigold's room carrying a tray loaded with pills and that disgusting chalky white liquid. Marigold could tell from the look in his eyes that he would tolerate no defiance from her. "My sweet, it's clear to me that I need to set some ground rules for you. First, you will take all these medications and drink all the elixir without choking or throwing up. If you repeat your foolishness of last night, I will have a doctor to come in and force a tube through your nose and down your throat into your stomach, and I promise you that the experience will be very unpleasant indeed. Do not make me resort to that, but I will if you insist on defying me." He picked up the first pill and the glass of liquid and handed it to her. Marigold wanted to throw it in his face, but the thought of someone forcing a tube through her nose terrified her, so she swallowed the pill and all the subsequent ones he gave her and drank all the vile liquid. Her stomach heaved with each sip, but she kept taking deeps breaths and was able to fight off the spasms. Shelton, or whatever his name was, smiled and kissed her on the lips just as if they were lovers. "You need not get dressed because I'll be back in two hours to transport you to another part of this facility. It's time for the next step in the procedure. Oh, my dear, people are going to read about you for generations to come. We're both going to be famous. You should be excited at the prospect."

CHAPTER 23

Gregg gave Barbara a call to tell her about the possible lead. Barbara put her phone on speaker so that Maryann could hear the conversation. "Mom, Rick was able to look at some footage from a surveillance camera at the health club, and he got a license plate number off the BMW that this Shelton guy drove away in after he and Marigold came back from having coffee on Friday. By the way, Goldie was sending us another clue when she referred to that actor Terrance Harris in her e-mail. Rick agrees with her that the guy does resemble him, at least in profile, although he didn't get a good frontal view. The guy evidently knew the cameras were there, and he seemed to very deliberately do things so his face couldn't be seen directly. We're hoping to get a better look at him from the surveillance cameras at Starbucks, but we probably won't be able to get access to that video footage until we get a subpoena. Anyway, after we got the plate number off the BMW, we pulled up some records from the Department of Motor Vehicles. The car is not registered to this Shelton guy. The information and DMV photo is for a Caucasian guy named Travis Mitchell, age fifty-nine. We went to his last known address, a high-rise downtown, only to find out that he vacated without notice a couple of weeks back. The apartment manager said that he left in such a hurry, he didn't even take time to recoup his security deposit. He'd been living there for about two years. He didn't leave a forwarding address, only a post office box somewhere in Missouri where he wanted his mail forwarded. We're following up on that too."

"Gregg, didn't the computer guy say that the IP address from Goldie's e-mail was in Missouri? There's got to be a connection. But now you're saying that you can't find this Travis Mitchell, so how does any of this even help us?"

"We haven't located him yet, Mom, but that doesn't mean that we won't. We've already issued an alert for law enforcement agencies to be on the lookout for the BMW. We're checking out the place of employment that Travis Mitchell listed on his apartment lease application. We're going to pull his phone records to see what direction that points us in. And we're still working on enhancing that photo Goldie's neighbor shot of the van that we believe was used in the abduction. According to the chief of security at the apartment where Travis was living, he was never seen driving the BMW—it was always a black SUV. My bet is that it's the same vehicle. All this is going to help us find this guy, and he's the key to finding Marigold."

"We're just so afraid, Gregg," said Maryann. "Mother's been gone approaching seventy-two hours now."

"I know, Maryann, but you have heard from her twice, and you know for sure that those messages were actually from her based on the information she put in them. So, she has been gone for almost seventy-two hours, but not out of communication for that long. I know it's hard, but you've got to hang in there and keep the faith. There are a lot of good people working on finding your mother, and I believe in them. I need you to believe in them too. Promise me you'll keep your chin up. Do it for your mother and for Amber too, okay?"

"I'll do my best, Gregg, and thank you for the pep talk. I needed it, and I feel a little better now that you guys have a few leads."

"Okay, Maryann. And, Mom, everything I said goes for you too. You just need to trust us to do our jobs. We're all good at it. I've got to get back to work now. I've got a few more things to check out. I'll be sure to update you every step of the way. Talk to you two later."

Maryann and Barbara gave each other a hug after they hung up with Gregg. They were both trying hard to be optimistic, but Maryann nervously kept checking her cell phone as if she could magically conjure up a call or a text message from her mother. Barbara kept checking her computer, hoping for another e-mail. There were no ticking clocks in Barbara's house. They were all digital. In their minds, however, both women could hear time ticking away, and they continued to worry.

CHAPTER 24

Hundreds of miles away from where Barbara and Maryann sat and worried, a heated discussion was taking place in the same building where Marigold sat and contemplated her future. The man known as Travis Mitchell was trying to convince the man known as Shelton Maxwell that it was foolhardy to proceed with the experimental protocol at this point. "I'm telling you that Marigold is not ready for the second injection yet. The first one I gave her was very small, only .5 cc and still I had to stop when her blood pressure began to climb so sharply. We need to give her at least another three doses of the prep. You seem to have forgotten what happened to the others. The first one started to seize immediately, and before we could stop her, she fell and cracked her head open. You do remember that, don't you, Shelton? Sometimes, you have a knack for developing selective amnesia. She was dead in less than five minutes, and we weren't equipped to do anything about it. You seem to think the blow to the head killed her. I disagree. I think injecting the solution directly into the vessels leading to her brain is what killed her. And I was left with the mess of cleaning up, of disposing of the body. The second one was an even worse disaster. A few hours after her first injection, her body went into total system failure. Fortunately, I have a very good friend who runs a crematorium, so I didn't have any problem getting rid of her body. I just faked a death certificate and told him she was an old friend who no longer had any family, and I was taking care of her last arrangements. He was glad to help, especially for twice the amount he would have charged anybody else. I paid it just in case your recklessness causes me to have to use him again."

"Travis, you are such a lily-livered coward," sneered Shelton. "That's probably why you couldn't hack it as a legitimate physician. Why I chose you to help me on my path to greatness is a mystery to me now, but since I've paid you a small fortune and made you privy to all my plans, we're stuck to each other like glue for the duration. Like I have told you time and time again, the reason we failed with the others is because their bodies were weakened, either from disease and malnutrition from living out in the streets, or from drugs or alcohol or other such abuses that street people indulge in. But I had to start somewhere to find human test subjects after my previous employer shut down my research, and based on what, based on the fact that some lab rats died? What garbage! The rats are expendables, that's why we use them."

"See, Shelton, again, you're only looking at half the picture. They weren't worried that the rats died. They were concerned that you couldn't tell them exactly why the rats died. They were concerned that your formula was too toxic to take a chance on human trials."

"They just didn't give me enough time to prove that my formula was viable," said Shelton. They are just a bunch of small-minded bureaucrats who can never see the big picture. Great medical progress means great sacrifices. I already had the human volunteers lined up. Isn't it great that some people will do anything for money, but New Generations found out about it and said that I had overstepped my boundaries, that I was unduly risking lives. They never seemed to care whose lives were at risk when I helped them develop the drugs that made them billionaires. But this time, when I was on the verge of the medical and scientific breakthrough of the millennium, they had to take the moral high ground and shut me down. So, I went out and found a few new volunteers, promised to pay them for a few days of their time. They came willingly, probably licking their chops over the prospect of having a few bucks for booze or drugs, and nobody even missed them. You see, Travis, nobody cares about those homeless people. Those women are better off dead."

"The difference here, Shelton," said Travis, "is that somebody does care about that woman, Marigold. She has a family. The cops are already looking for her. Your little ruse with the e-mail didn't work as well as *you thought. The source I paid off at the apartment I was renting called me on my throwaway cell this afternoon. The cops are looking for me. Probably because you used the BMW that happens to be registered to me. I told you to be careful, but you are such an arrogant prick that you never listen to me. You think you can get away with anything. One of these days, you're going to walk so close to the edge of the abyss that you're going to slip and go over."*

"I like living on the edge, Travis, it excites me, and so do you. Isn't that what gambling is all about? Besides, I could hardly seduce a woman like Marigold driving around in something as mundane as a Ford or Chevy, now, could I? And my own luxury cars would have drawn far too much attention. I learned a lot about this woman from the questionnaire she filled out for Fountain of Youth, then I read her profile on eHarmony. The rest was online research, including a little hacking into forbidden databases. People just don't realize what kind of information about themselves is floating around in cyberspace. Then I did some subtle stalking. I found out where she and her friend like to shop, what kinds of food she likes to eat, what day of the month she gets her social security direct deposit, how much money she has in the bank, which is quite substantial by the way, and how much she owes on her credit cards. Hell, I even know the name of her hair stylist. I knew she was the perfect subject, and I also knew exactly what buttons to push to get Marigold to trust me. My sweet little cougar was ripe for the picking, missing her dead husband, but wanting to get it on with a younger man. She was putty in my hands, especially after I added my special formula to her coffee. She really is very sexy, you know, and I love women who remind me of my mother. I should have gotten a little taste of her before I started the protocol."

"You really are a sicko, Shelton, you know that? But the bigger question right now is, what makes you think that Marigold is going to survive, even if she is a healthier specimen than the others?"

"I told you, Travis, that I have eliminated much of the toxic qualities of the elixir, and I'm using a quite different variation of the human growth hormone. It worked splendidly with the last batch of rats. After only a week, several of the oldest ones started to run around with new energy and act young again. It was amazing how much sex they were having. That was the only bad side effect—some of them sexed each other

to death. On autopsy, their brains looked vastly different from earlier brain scans. The plaque inside the blood vessels and other signs of aging had lessened in some of the rats and was completely gone in others. You understand what that means, Travis, I actually succeeded in reversing aging in some of those rats!"

"But, Shelton, all the rats died within two months. How can you say that it worked 'splendidly,' as you describe it? And you still can't tell definitively why the rats died. I know one thing you did see in the autopsies that you can't explain—that strange luminosity in the brain tissue. I still say that the elixir, as you prefer to call it, is toxic as hell, and I think you need to proceed very carefully to avoid killing Marigold. And that's another thing, even if by chance she doesn't die right away and you get a chance to document your results, what are you going to do with her then, kill her yourself? Because I certainly won't do it. I got rid of those other bodies for you, but I will not commit cold-blooded murder for you. You can't pay me enough for that. Marigold knows you kidnapped her, and she can certainly identify you. You had already sedated her when we put her in the van, so she never saw me. You think she'll be so grateful to you for erasing a few lines from her face and revving up her libido that she'll forgive you and let you go on your merry way? Without your test subject alive and well and growing younger, no one will ever believe in the credibility of your work. You'll retire to some obscure place all right, but it'll be because you'll be running from the law the rest of your days. And your hopes of being published in research and medical journals and winning a Nobel prize—forget it, it'll never happen."

"I will do what I have to do, and whatever fate befalls Marigold will be in the name of the progress of medical science, something many have died for. And yes, she will be grateful to me for not only giving her a new lease on life, making her look and feel better, and also making it possible for her to live for who knows how long. For all you know, she may choose to share her life with me. I've already given her a taste of a little formula I developed, which makes me quite irresistible to women. Once my little Marigold has been infused with the final dose of elixir, I'll just give her a periodic taste of my special liquid. She won't want to leave my presence. When they find out what I've accomplished, the medical community may not publicly acknowledge it, but they will be in awe *of my discovery, and their public views will not keep me from becoming filthy rich. Ever hear of the black market? Methuselah wannabes will be knocking down my door to buy the formula. Even some of those doctors who would publicly shun me will be trying to gain access."*

"There's another thing I don't understand, Shelton, why did you let that Weiss woman go into Marigold's room? Now there's another person who has seen her. If she opens her mouth—"

"Travis, you are treading into dangerous waters. Don't ever question my actions. Marva is my business, and I assure you that I can handle her. She doesn't even know my real last name, only the Marshall alias I use here. The only time she'll open her mouth is to scream out her pleasure when I'm making love to her. She was a little cool when I first met her, didn't want to get it on the first time we dated, but after I sweetened her wine with my something special, she practically tore my clothes off. I'm her Adonis, her dream come true. Marigold thinks Marva is a doctor. Marva thinks Marigold is a nut. A sweet little joke on the both of them, if you ask me.

"Now, I am really tired of this discussion, Travis, and we will proceed on schedule to give Marigold the next injection—a full dose this time. You have it ready by six o'clock, and I don't want to hear any more of your whinny excuses. And in the future, I would appreciate it if you would dispense with the morality lectures. At least I'm doing what I do for a noble purpose. Your motivation, on the other hand, is purely selfishness and greed. You want to keep big bucks coming into your pockets to enable your quite expensive gambling escapades and to indulge your appetite for high-class call girls."

That guy is becoming more and more unhinged, *thought Travis as the door slammed behind Shelton. He's literally and figuratively turning into a "mad scientist."* The guy hadn't seemed crazy when they had first formed a partnership. How could he have known that he was about to climb into bed with the devil? They were both out of a job after that unfortunate incident in Green River caused the spa to go bankrupt. After all, who would want to be a guest at a so-called health spa where people died in a sauna, for God's sake. For a long time now, Travis had harbored a sneaking suspicion that those two women had been Shelton's first experiments. Shelton told him that he was doing some research on a drug *that would be a huge breakthrough in geriatric medicine, a drug that would make billions of dollars. He said he needed someone like Travis to be his assistant, someone who could be discreet and wouldn't mind pushing a few envelopes. Travis wondered, for the umpteenth time in the last few months, how he had allowed himself to get in such deep muck. He knew the answer, of course; Shelton was right, it was because he had let his greed get the better of him. He didn't exactly know where Shelton's money came from; he suspected that the man was cooking up designer drugs for his well-heeled users, but it didn't really matter to him as long as the pay was good. Travis liked the lifestyle the money had afforded him. He liked playing the tables in Vegas, so much in fact that his formerly fat bank account had slimmed down considerably; he liked the gorgeous high-class call girls who were at his beck and call if the price was right; he loved driving fancy cars. Damn that Shelton, the BMW had been his favorite and he'd had to order one of his cohorts to get rid of it, told the guy to burn it to the ground. Who knows what kind of forensic evidence the authorities might have found in the car. If it wasn't for the dwindling status of his bank account, and for the fact that he was afraid of Shelton, Travis would have packed it in by now, gotten out while the getting was good. His biggest mistake to date was getting involved in Marigold Robbins's kidnapping. There was no evidence linking him to the deaths of those homeless women. But together, he and Shelton had transported the Robbins woman over state lines, and Travis knew that if the FBI somehow got involved, they were screwed. The FBI was a dangerous and persistent adversary. Once they started after you, they didn't quit.*

"This is the last time that I'm getting involved in Shelton's schemes," said Travis to himself. He had made up his mind that he was going to take whatever funds he had left and put as much distance between him and Shelton as possible. And it was going to be somewhere without an extradition treaty with the United States, just in case. He put all those depressing thoughts out of his head, got the necessary materials out of the lab freezer, and busied himself preparing a potentially lethal injection for Marigold, just like a good little minion.

CHAPTER 25

Rick did an Internet search for *New Generations*. He found a listing for a biomedical research corporation that specialized in research in geriatric pharmacology. According to literature in the journals of the *American Geriatric Society*, the company had several years ago been involved in the potential development of a line of drugs that were supposedly more effective in treating the "geriatric giants" (immobility, instability, incontinence, and impaired intellect/memory) with fewer harmful side effects than the traditional drugs that had been on the market for years. The main source of funding for this research was in the form of a research grant from the Geriatric Medicine Department of the University of Virginia. For some reason, about two years ago, the research funding had been withdrawn. Rick called the telephone number he pulled from the website for New Generations and got a message saying, "The number you have reached is no longer in service." He found a directory listing for the building address shown on the Web. The research company was no longer listed as a tenant. Evidently, New Generations had gone belly up after the university stopped the grant money. He needed to talk to somebody over there to see if he could find out why, and more importantly, to see if he could find a connection to Travis Mitchell.

Rick decided to call the University of Virginia Hospital to see if he could find out who he needed to talk to regarding the now-defunct New Generations research grant. He was told that the geriatric medicine administrative offices were closed this morning because of a special board meeting that most of the staff were required to attend, so there were no staff members available who could tell him the name of the person he needed to talk to. Rick hung up and went back to his true and tried source of information—the Internet.

After several false starts, he finally found a website that listed the names of "grant fund administrators" for the University of Virginia Hospital. He was astounded at the number of names —there were about twenty (it was actually called a board of administrators). Most of them had a bunch of initials following their names signifying their medical degrees and specialties. One was a CPA and one was an attorney. Four of the doctors' names were shown in bold print, so Rick decided to start with them. He used a telephone directory system to locate phone numbers and home addresses for the four. He hoped he could get them on the phone because all the home addresses, except one, were at least two to three hours away. He called the number with the local address first, belonging to a Dr. Raheem Patel, using the station phone instead of his cell so the caller ID on the other end would alert the answerer that he was calling from the Albemarle County Police Department and was not just an "unknown caller."

The phone was picked up on the third ring, and a woman, probably a Hispanic domestic, said, "Hello, *hola*, this is the residence of Dr. and Mrs. Patel."

"Hello, ma'am, my name is Rick Williams, and I am a police detective with the Albemarle County Police Department. I need to speak to Dr. Patel on an urgent matter."

"I am sorry, senor," said the woman, "but Dr. Patel he is not at home now."

"What about Mrs. Patel?"

"No, senor, Mrs. Patel, she is away also."

"Is there any way you can get in touch with the doctor and give him a message to return my call? As I said, it is extremely urgent that I speak with him just as soon as possible."

"Yes, I theenk it is possible to do for you, senor, since you are with the police. Dr. Patel, he gives me emergency numbers in case something needs his attention when he is away. I cannot give you the number, but I can try to call Dr. Patel as you have said and give him your number."

"Thank you, ma'am," said Rick. "Please write down these numbers. Tell him he should try calling my cell phone first as I may be away from the station when he gets back to me." He read the numbers and had the woman verify that she had them right. And what is your name, ma'am?"

"My name is Rosa Esposito, Mr. Williams, I am housekeeper to Dr. Patel and Mrs. Patel."

"You've been very helpful, Ms. Esposito. Again, I thank you." Rick hung up the phone and waited. He passed the time by continuing to peruse the Internet listings for "fountain of youth." Twenty minutes later, his cell phone rang. It was Dr. Patel. "Detective Williams, I presume you have a very good reason for having Mrs. Esposito disrupt my golf game. I can only give you a few minutes. I'm on the sixteenth green, and I'm on the verge of shooting a lower score than my partners, so this had better be good."

"I do apologize, Dr. Patel," said Rick. "Under ordinary circumstances, I wouldn't think of interfering with anyone's leisure activities, but this matter is very urgent. Let me explain. I am investigating the disappearance and probable abduction of an Albemarle County resident by the name of Marigold Robbins. We don't think she was kidnapped for money. We've had no ransom demands, but the case has some very disturbing elements in it. We believe this woman's life is in imminent danger. I called you because, in the course of the investigation, we discovered that on the day she went missing, she was seen in a vehicle, a silver-colored BMW to be specific, that we traced to an employee of a biomedical research company called New Generations. It's my understanding that they formerly worked on some research under a grant from the University of Virginia."

"New Generations," interjected Dr. Patel. "Yes, that's the firm whose grant we had to withdraw about two years ago. I don't think they're in business any longer. But look, Detective Williams, it sounds like this could get complicated. I don't mean to sound crass, but I'm going to have to call you back in, say, forty-five minutes after I finish my round. I'm backing people up here, and they get very testy when they're held up on a golf course that costs them three hundred dollars to play eighteen holes. I'm sure you understand."

"Actually, I can't say that I do, Doctor," said Rick testily. "Given the urgency of this situation, but hey, I did interrupt your game, so I'll be waiting to hear back from you." After he hung up, Rick berated himself for being so short with Dr. Patel. He needed the man's cooperation; being antagonistic was not exactly the way to get it. When Dr. Patel called back an hour later, Rick apologized to him. "Look, Doc, I'm sorry I snapped at you the first time we talked. Chalk it up to too much coffee and too little sleep the last forty-eight hours or so. I'm really anxious to find Mrs. Robbins and bring her home safely to her family."

"No offense taken, Detective," said Dr. Patel. "Maybe you should try golf—being out there on the course can sometimes be a tremendous stress reliever, then there are all those other times," he laughed. "Seriously, how do you think I can help you?"

"As I started to explain earlier, Doctor Patel, this past Friday, Mrs. Robbins was seen riding in a silver-colored BMW with a license plate registered to one Travis Mitchell. We know this because we had a video tape showing the plate number. A Department of Motor Vehicles database led us to his last known address. The man was gone, whereabouts unknown, but the lease records from the apartment he occupied for two years prior listed New Generations as his employer. An Internet search of *New Generations* revealed that the company, a biomedical research outfit, was no longer in business, but I subsequently pulled up some information on the research grant first issued, then withdrawn, by the University of Virginia. That's how I ended up interrupting your golf game. Your name was listed—in bold print, I might add—as one of the grant fund administrators for the university. Anything you can tell me about New Generations might help me to find Travis Mitchell. We know another man is involved, but so far, Mitchell is the only person we've actually identified."

"Well, there is not really much that I can tell you. I can only speak in generalities as to the nature of the research that was being done because some of the information is proprietary. You see, some drug companies also put up money for the grant. The company was involved in clinical research on certain drugs appropriate for treating the elderly. I am prohibited from specifying the exact kinds and purposes of the drugs. What I can tell you is that we terminated our portion of the grant when we found out that the company was not following Food and Drug Administration guidelines for testing. They were walking a thin line when it came to human subject testing, and we could not afford to have them cross over the line with us involved. The guidelines for such testing is very specific and very stringent. Any protocol irregularities could get us into deep trouble with the FDA. Our money represented two-thirds of the research funding. Once we pulled out, the project was doomed to fail."

"Dr. Patel, did you know Travis Mitchell personally, or any other individual that worked for New Generations?" asked Rick.

"No, Detective, as one of the chief fund administrators—those people listed in bold print—I don't get involved in the details. We read reports and oversee expenditures. I'm pretty sure I can have a staff member get you personnel lists and other data relating to New Generations. However, I'll need to consult our attorneys first to make sure I'm not violating any legalities. Take down this name and numbers." Dr. Patel gave him the name and office, home, and cell numbers of a staff member who had access to the files they had talked about. "I'll call someone from our legal department to make sure I'm not overstepping, and I'll get back to you to give you the okay to go ahead and talk to Shelly Madison. Heaven help me if my attorney is on the golf course; he's not nearly as forgiving as I am. I'll pave the way with Shelly, and tell her you need the information stat. I hope you find that poor woman."

"Thank you, Dr. Patel," said Rick. "I'll let you know what shakes out. Good luck on your future golf games."

CHAPTER 26

Gregg looked at his watch; he could hardly believe that it was already three o'clock in the afternoon. In a couple of hours, it would be seventy-two hours since Marigold had vanished. He had just gotten back into the station when he got a call from Harold, the computer technician, asking him to come over; he had some information about the SUV. He said he had called Rick, but his phone had gone directly to voice mail. Gregg looked over at the desk the detective was using just as Rick was hanging up from talking to Dr. Patel. He motioned him over, and they caught the elevator to the fifth floor where the computer lab was located. On the way up, Rick briefed Gregg on his progress with New Generations and Travis Mitchell.

Harold was sitting at his computer, as usual, when Rick and Gregg walked in. They wondered if the guy even had a life outside of cyberspace. Empty Styrofoam coffee cups were lined up like sentinels on a nearby bookcase. "You ever go home, buddy?" teased Rick.

"What for?" said Harold. "I've got everything I need right here: a toothbrush, a cot to sleep on, and plenty of stale coffee. Who could ask for more?" He punched some keys on his computer, pulled up some images, and directed their attention to a fifty-inch monitor on the wall. "I played around with Flossie's smart phone photo, and this is what I got," he said.

Rick was surprised at the clarity of the enhanced picture, given how it had looked on Flossie's phone. It was a black Chrysler Aspen SUV, the 2001 model, according to Harold—its license plate number now visible, thanks to the computer tech's magic. It was a Virginia plate. The sticker that Flossie had seen on the back window was a parking permit, number G21010, but no indication of who had issued the permit. Harold had run the plates through the Department of Motor Vehicles database; it came up as a fleet car registered to New Generations Biotechnical Laboratories. The registration was expired. The logo was a picture of a garden fountain.

"Hold on Harold," said Gregg. "You said that the SUV is a 2001 model. Are you sure?"

"Does a chicken have legs? Of course, I'm sure."

"Damn, then that means it's not the same vehicle that Travis Mitchell had parked in the garage. The security guy said it was a late model, 2008 or 2009."

Rick could make out some tiny writing at the left edge of the picture. "Harold, is there any way you can make that part of the image larger so we can read what it says on the fountain picture?"

"Your wish is my command," said the technician, clicking keys as he was speaking. The part of the image Rick wanted enlarged first appeared in a tiny box. Harold manipulated keys on his keyboard and—voila—visible words appeared on the screen. "Fountain of Youth Medical Spa and Health Farms."

"Let's see where this leads us," said Harold as he quickly typed in several commands on his keyboard. On the large monitor, in a split-screen mode, several articles popped up at once. Rick and Gregg began to scan the first one, which, in chronological order, was actually the last one.

GREEN RIVER STAR
November 20, 2003

WRONGFUL DEATH SUIT DISMISSED FOR LACK OF EVIDENCE

The wrongful death action filed twenty-two months ago against the Fountain of Youth Spa and Health Farm was dismissed by Judge Felicia

Jackson, citing lack of evidence to proceed. The families of the two victims—Emily Cook, age sixty-five, and Elizabeth Procter, age sixty-nine—said they plan to appeal the judge's ruling. The two women died under what the families described as "mysterious" circumstances at the spa in the summer of 2001. The spa is no longer in business, filing for bankruptcy last year.

The second article was similar:

GREEN RIVER STAR
January 2002

SUIT FILED AGAINST FOUNTAIN OF YOUTH

Two families, alleging wrongful death of relatives, filed suit in Wyoming yesterday against the Fountain of Youth Medical Spa and Health Farm. The spa was run by a man by the name of Shawn Elton Maxwell. The daughter of Emily Cook and the husband of Elizabeth Proctor claim that the women had entered a contest where they won a two-week, all-expense paid trip to the spa and health farm, located in the desert near Green River. The two women did not know each other. Emily Cook was a resident of New York City, and Elizabeth Proctor resided in Chicago, Illinois. The women were both found dead in a sauna-like room. After they missed several appointments scheduled for later that day, spa personnel initiated a search and found the women unconscious in the room. All efforts to revive them failed. They were unclothed, but robes and towels were found nearby. The deaths were investigated, autopsies were performed, and the medical examiner determined that the women died of heat stroke, with underlying medical conditions as contributing factors. No negligence on the part of the spa was cited because the sauna was inspected and found to meet all applicable safety standards. The families disagreed with the findings, stating that the women were in good health before they went to the spa and that neither was under a doctor's care or on any medications for any "underlying medical conditions." Proctor's husband had an independent autopsy performed on his wife, and the pathologist says he found strange striations in Elizabeth's brain, origin unknown, which could have caused seizure activity, possibly causing her to lose consciousness while in the sauna. He claims to have talked to his wife on the morning of the day she died and that she told him she had felt ill the day before after a spa treatment of some kind, but gave no details. Emily Cook's family verified that she also had complained of feeling unwell. The spa management had no comment on the suit other than to deny any liability in the deaths of the women.

*****

GREEN RIVER STAR
July 15, 2001

WOMEN FOUND DEAD IN DESERT SAUNA

Two women, both in their sixties, were pronounced dead yesterday after they were discovered in a sauna at a popular Green River health spa. The women were guests at the facility. Local authorities are investigating what they are calling "suspicious deaths." Autopsies are pending. The spa has been ordered closed by the state health department until the investigation into the deaths has been completed.

After reading the articles, wheels started turning in Rick's head. He didn't much believe in coincidence and had his own philosophy about it: two coincidences could be chalked up to happenstance—maybe—but three coincidences spelled c-o-n-s-p-i-r-a-c-y, and there were far too many popping up here; too many suspicious deaths involving women in their sixties.

"Harold, can you possibly get into any databases that might contain personnel records for that health spa? We need to know if Travis Mitchell was an employee there. If he was, I think that he could have been one of the men that Flossie saw in that van. The black van is linked to both Fountain of Youth and to New Generations, and the BMW links Travis to our mystery man. Marigold was accessing a Fountain of Youth website on her computer before she went missing, and all evidence points to her having been abducted by this Terrance Howard look-alike, perhaps with the help of Travis Mitchell." Rick was thinking that the jigsaw puzzle pieces just might be starting to fill in.

Harold kept up a running conversation while he was working his magic on his keyboard. "Well, instead of searching all over the place trying to find some private records for the company you're looking at, let's go to places I know I can access. Everybody that runs a business like the Fountain of Youth, where they hire a number of employees and pay them a salary must pay payroll taxes to the government. I can get into a database that lists all the employees for whom Fountain of Youth paid taxes to the Feds. Just give me a sec."

In another thirty seconds, a list of names appeared on the big screen. Harold scrolled down and highlighted the name *Travis Barnwell Mitchell.* His job title was listed as "certified health coach." Harold punched some buttons on the keyboard, and the list materialized as a hard copy from the printer, which he handed to Rick.

"What the hell is a certified health coach?" said Rick. "I'm not familiar with that one."

"Maybe it's like a personal trainer or a motivator or something, you know, to teach you how to get healthy," said Harold. "But I can't say for sure man. Me, I've never even tried to get healthy. I drink, smoke, eat a lot of red meat, never touch a piece of lettuce or a carrot, and I look at dirty movies. I might die young, but I'll die happy."

"You know, Harold," said Gregg laughing, "there is something definitely wrong with you. You need to stay off that computer. I think it's scrambling your brain."

"Do one last thing for me, Harold," said Rick. "Then I'll let you get back to your other work. I know you've spent quite a bit of time looking up stuff for us. When we pulled up Department of Motor Vehicles records for the BMW, we didn't find any other vehicles registered to Travis Mitchell. The thing is, we know for sure that he was driving around in a late-model SUV, because that's the car he parked in his assigned space in the apartment garage, so it must be registered under some other name. Maybe the vehicle belongs to somebody else and Mitchell was just using it, but I find it hard to believe that you can borrow somebody's car every day for two years. Could be he's married and is using his wife's car, but my gut is telling me otherwise. Why don't we try playing around with the name, putting in some variations of his name and see if we get anything. Try Travis Barnwell or Mitchell Barnwell or Barnwell Mitchell and see if you get a hit."

Harold clicked a few keys, and a DMV record with the name Travis Barnwell appeared on the screen. He was the registered owner of a 2009 Chrysler Aspen SUV. His address was the same as the one that had been listed for Travis Mitchell. His DMV photo was the same. It was the same man. But knowing this information was not going to help Marigold. It was a dead end.

Gregg promised Harold that he would bring him the promised six-pack as soon as he could sneak it in. He couldn't openly bring alcohol into a police station, but he wanted to show Harold his appreciation for all his help. Rick's cell phone rang just as they were getting off the elevator to return to Gregg's work station. It was Dr. Patel.

"Hello, Doctor," said Rick. "I hope you have some news for me."

"Yes, Detective, I have consulted our grants attorney—who was not on the golf course, by the way—and he has no problem with allowing you access to the personnel records for New Generations. I have passed the word along to Shelly Madison, so just give her a call. You already have her number. Just give her your e-mail address, and she will send you the records. They will be limited to information regarding personnel of New Generations only. Any information concerning the research itself will have been deleted. I hope this will be of help."

"Thank you very much, Dr. Patel," said Rick. "I'll call Ms. Madison right away." He clicked off and pulled out the Post-it note that he had used to jot down Shelly Madison's number. She picked up on the first ring.

"Hello, this is Shelly Madison, may I help you?" Rick identified himself, and Shelly told him that she had the records ready. He gave her the e-mail address for Gregg's computer at the station. In a few minutes, Gregg's computer signaled that he had incoming mail. Gregg opened the message and directed it to the printer. He printed out a copy for each of them. It was a complete list of every employee at New Generations that was assigned to work on the clinical research team for the University of Virginia Grant project, including their job titles and job descriptions and some background information on each of them.

Rick perused the list of some twenty-five names and, sure enough, Travis Mitchell was listed as an employee. His job title said that he was a "research assistant." Another name caught his eye. He quickly pulled out the list of personnel for the Fountain of Youth Spa and Health Farm and ran his hand down the list. "Hey, Gregg, take a look at this. There's another name in common on both these lists. The guy that ran the health spa was named Shawn Elton Maxwell. And here on the personnel roster for New Generations, the chief clinical researcher is a guy named S. Elton Maxwell. You can't tell me that he's not one and the same." Rick got Shelly Madison on the phone. "I hate to bother you again, Ms. Madison, but I have another question. Did the New Generations people have access to the labs and facilities at the University of Virginia when they were involved in the research, and if so, did the university take photos for the purposes of issuing identification badges? They did, that is good to hear. Can you possibly send me photos of two of those people: S. Elton Maxwell and Travis Mitchell. Yes, my computer is still turned on, so direct the photos to the same e-mail address you used when you sent me the personnel list."

A few minutes, the computer signaled incoming e-mail. Rick opened the message and waited for the photos to open. One picture matched the DMV photo of Travis Mitchell; the other photo was a dead ringer for the actor Terrance Harris. *Gotcha*, thought Rick. *We know who you are, now we've just got to find you!*

CHAPTER 27

Somewhere in the Ozarks, Travis Mitchell was preparing the elixir for injection into Marigold. He was so engrossed in his work, or either the lab was so well insulated, that he didn't hear the rumbling of thunder some distance away and then growing closer and louder. A storm was brewing in the mountains. Suddenly, without warning, the lights blinked out, and the room went dark. This was formerly a full-service medical facility equipped with backup power, so emergency generators would turn the lights back on within twenty seconds of an electrical outage. The problem was that the sudden dousing of light so startled Travis that his hand struck one of the vials of fluid sitting on the bench next to him. As the generators kicked in and the lights came back on, Travis watched in a kind of horrid fascination as a crucial component of Shelton's precious elixir pooled on the floor amid the shattered glass of the vial that had contained it. Oh, damn, Shelton will have a coronary, *he thought,* and he will most certainly take out his wrath on me. The component that was spoiled was the buffer. Without the buffering agent, he might as well inject the woman with battery acid. He needed at least two hours for more of the element to percolate, but the dose was supposed to be ready for Marigold at six o'clock, which was a little less than forty-five minutes from now. Travis's mind was frantically scrambling to come up with a solution to his dilemma. Shelton was a marvelous researcher, but he was no doctor. Travis decided that he could deceive him this one time. He would bring the woman in and watch Travis inject her with the liquid. Didn't he say that he believed that the stuff was no longer toxic? So, he wouldn't* be suspicious if Marigold didn't show any immediate adverse reaction to the injection. There was no way he would know that the hypodermic was filled with something else, as long as it looked the same. In a few hours, Travis could replace the needed component. Shelton would be looking for clinical indicators that the stuff was working, and he would insist on blood work to verify any changes in hormone levels, but Travis would be the one to document the changes. He was sure he could fake the results temporarily. He quickly cleaned up the evidence of the spill and readied a hypodermic with a harmless solution. He was nervous and hoped his nervousness didn't give him away. He hated to admit that he was afraid of the man, but he had concluded that Shelton Maxwell was completely insane. The phone rang. Travis knew who it was before he answered.

"Travis, I wanted to make sure everything is still on schedule and that nothing was affected by the momentary power failure." Travis assured him that everything was just fine and dandy. He found some paper towel and wiped off the sweat that had accumulated on his forehead.

Marigold had a moment of sheer panic when the lights went out, but seconds later, they came back on. She had been listening to the developing storm for the past hour. She even went over to the window and pulled the drapes back as the lightening flashed high above the mountains. She wondered if this was the last time she would witness a thunderstorm. She tried not to think morbid thoughts, but she couldn't help herself. Her last will and testament was in the safety deposit box at her bank. Both Barbara and Maryann had a key. She had enough money in the bank to pay off all her outstanding debts and to leave a legacy for her grandchild should she not survive. She wondered if anyone would ever find her body. As she thought about her family and her best friend, tears filled her eyes. She impatiently brushed them away. Tears of self-pity could not help her now. She had to hope that the police or the FBI or somebody was looking for her and that they would find her in time. Marigold didn't know what time it was, but she felt that it was nearing the time when Shelton said that he would come for her so he could perform "the procedure," whatever it was. She waited and prayed.

CHAPTER 28

Rick and Gregg were scrambling to find out any and everything they could on Shawn Elton Maxwell. They discovered that the man had a PhD in clinical research that he had obtained from the University of California at San Francisco, as well as a master's degree in psychiatry. He had been a researcher with one of the giant pharmaceuticals at the same time he was listed as head of the Fountain of Youth Health Spa, but he had been terminated by the drug company shortly thereafter, possibly because of the adverse publicity of the deaths in the desert. He then signed on with New Generations, a fledgling biomedical research corporation, and was instrumental in developing a new geriatric drug that sold remarkably well and put New Generations on the map. His last known address was the same local hotel listed for Travis Mitchell prior to Mitchell leasing the apartment he had just vacated. IRS records showed that same address. They searched all the phone records for any calls made to and from Shawn Elton Maxwell when he was in the employ of New Generations. The calls received at the research facility appeared legitimate. Other calls were to a pre-paid, throwaway cell phone, that could not be tied to an address. The Virginia Department of Motor Vehicles had no record of any vehicle registered to Shawn Elton Maxwell or S. Elton Maxwell. Neither did any other DMV in the United States. If the guy drove a car, it was one that was not one registered in his own name. He had no family, at least none that they could find, and they could find no record of any bank accounts in local banks under his name and social security number. They also could not find credit cards in his name. The man either did everything by proxy, or he was a freaking ghost. Rick and Gregg were beyond frustrated.

Gregg went into his commander's office and gave him an update on the progress of the investigation. At last the man's interest was finally piqued. "You got any other possible leads on this guy?" he asked.

"Well, we're still trying to contact this Charlie, the maintenance guy he was seen conferring with at the apartment building where the alleged accomplice was staying. He's not answering his phone though, and Rick and I are much too busy right now to spend two hours driving out to his address."

"I'll send a couple uniforms to see if he's home. If he isn't, they can stick around for a while to see if he shows up. What else can I do?"

"You can notify your counterpart in Chicago that we've identified the guy that belongs to a fingerprint in a cold case they had a while back. It looked like a homicide to them, but they didn't have any leads. Get them involved. We need all the help we can get. I suppose we can't get the FBI, can we, since we can't prove that Mrs. Robbins has been kidnapped for sure or that she has been transported across state lines."

"It's doubtful, Gregg, but since I've been less than helpful to you on this up until now, I'll reach out to some friends to see what can be done. They do have resources we don't have."

As Gregg got up to leave, the commander's phone rang. He held up his hand and motioned for him to wait. "Yes, I'll let him know. Tell them to rush any results. A woman's life may be at stake here." When the commander ended the call, he turned to Gregg. "Gregg, they found the BMW. It was overturned down an embankment in a heavily wooded area off the freeway. There's a dead body inside. Crime scene techs transmitted fingerprints directly to the crime lab. It's amazing what they can do with technology today. We don't even have to wait until the guys come back in to get an identification. The prints came back a match to one Charles Evans, your maintenance man from the hotel. Guess your interview with him is canceled. The medical examiner has to get him back to the morgue for an autopsy to determine cause of death, but he says that preliminary indications point toward him sustaining fatal injuries in the car crash. He wasn't wearing a seat belt, and his head went through the windshield. Because there was a BOLO on the vehicle, we are treating the accident site as a crime scene. The techs are processing the car right now. I told them we need the results ASAP."

Gregg went to tell Rick the bad news. "Man, everywhere we turn, we hit a brick wall. Charlie Evans bought the farm. He was driving the BMW that was registered to Travis Mitchell when he went off the freeway, down an embankment. He was pronounced dead at the scene. At least now we know for sure that he was somehow connected to Travis, or else why would he be driving the guy's car?"

"I've got an idea," said Rick. "And I don't know if it's good or bad. What if we turn the heat up on these guys? Somebody might have seen Goldie. We need to get her name and image out there, and I don't mean just locally. We need people to see her, and we need to offer a reward. The only thing sometimes that may backfire—you know, cause a perp to get rid of a victim. But we're at the seventy-two-hour mark, and we haven't heard any more from Marigold. We're finding out more and more about these creeps, but we still don't have a clue as to where to look for them. We need to go to your mom's place and talk to her and Maryann. I wouldn't want to do this without their approval. What do you think?"

"You're right, man, we're at our wits' end here, but I don't know if I like what you are proposing. However, I'll defer to Maryann and my mom on this. If you're ready, let's go."

Barbara heard Gregg first knock then put his key in the lock as he let himself into her house. He wasn't smiling, and she braced herself for what she thought was bad news.

"Mom, we finally identified the man who took Marigold. His name is Shawn Elton Maxwell, but these days, he's calling himself Shelton Maxwell."

Barbara hadn't realized that she was holding her breath until she exhaled sharply after Gregg started speaking. "Who is this Shawn or Shelton, and why did he kidnap Goldie?"

"We're not sure, Mom, but we do know that he's a clinical researcher who last worked for a biomedical research group by the name of New Generations. New Generations apparently went belly up after research grant money was withdrawn by the University of Virginia because of some irregularities in the research. The powers that be at the university refuse to tell us what those irregularities were, but we suspect that it might have had something to do with human testing of the drugs they were developing. We also haven't been able to get the university to tell us specifically what the research was for, but we do know that New Generations was doing some cutting-edge development of drugs for geriatric pharmacology. Both this guy and Travis Mitchell, also known as Travis Barnwell—who we think is the other guy that Flossie saw in the van in the alley behind Marigold's house—worked for New Generations. The problem is, we can't locate either of these men. Shelton has no current address, no family that we could find, no vehicle registration, no credit cards issued in his name, and no traceable cell phone. We couldn't find any bank accounts either. He must have his money deposited in an offshore bank somewhere. He and Travis Mitchell seem to have vanished into thin air."

"What about that car you told us about," said Maryann. "That BMW, are the police still looking for it? Maybe that can lead you to my mother. There's got to be something." It was obvious that Maryann was near the breaking point.

"The car was found about two hours ago, Maryann, in a ditch off the freeway. The man who was driving it is dead. It wasn't either of the men we're looking for. We know that the dead man, Charlie Evans, knew Travis Mitchell. He was seen talking to him on several occasions at the apartment he was leasing."

Rick spoke up at that point. "Ladies, there's something else I haven't told you up to now, because I knew it would stress you out even more than you already are. We got a hit on the fingerprint from the Starbucks cup that was left in Marigold's Lexus before we even identified who the print belonged. Brace yourselves before I tell you this. The print came off a plastic hospital-like identification band wrapped around the wrist of a dead body, a Jane Doe in her sixties, found in Chicago two years ago. There was no name of any kind on the ID band, just a series of numbers. The woman was probably one of Chicago's homeless population because she appeared malnourished and was dressed in layers of clothing like homeless people tend to do. She is believed to have died of blunt force trauma to the back of the head, which would make it a homicide because people don't usually whack themselves in the back of their own heads. The reason I said 'believed' is because the medical examiner found something strange in the woman's brain, which no one to date has been able to identify. I'm not saying this to scare you, but this Shelton is a very dangerous man, and he may well be a murderer too."

Maryann was sobbing, loudly, and Barbara put her arms around her godchild to comfort and calm her.

Rick continued, "The reason I am telling you all of this now is because I need to ask you if we can go public with what happened to Marigold. Someone may have seen her or the abductors. We can plaster their faces all over the media too. The problem is that dangerous men like these may be willing to get rid of anybody who can identify them or lead the authorities to them. I need to know if you both are willing to take that chance, or in the alternative, take the chance that we're going to be able to find her before she is harmed. Either way, I know it's a tough decision, but I believe we're running out of time, and I wanted to give you a chance to decide before this matter is taken out of my hands."

"Rick, be straight with me," said Barbara. "Are you're saying is that you think this guy might have kidnapped Goldie to do some kind of experiments on her? That's just plain crazy."

"Yes, I agree, Barbara, it does sound crazy. And I'm not saying that Shelton is experimenting on Marigold. What I know for a fact is that his fingerprint was found in connection with a cold case where an elderly woman died under circumstances that are a little strange, and I know for a fact that Shelton was lingering around women of Goldie's age for a while, probably trying to pick the right victim—a candidate of his choosing—and I know for a fact that this same guy worked for a health spa called the

Fountain of Youth back in 2001 where two women, both in their sixties, were found dead under suspicious circumstances. Is it a coincidence that Goldie was looking at a website called Fountain of Youth on her computer? You might think so, but I don't believe in coincidence. And lastly, I'm been working this job long enough to know that people who go to great pains to erase all information about their whereabouts don't want anyone to know where they are because they are hiding something."

"So, now you want us to give Mother's picture to television stations," said Maryann. "But because these men are dangerous, you think doing that could possibly get my mother killed. But on the other hand, you think if we don't find her soon, she could still be killed. So, we're stuck between a rock and a hard place."

"I'm sorry, Maryann, but regretfully, that about sums it up," said Rick. "If you do decide to go public, you might want to offer a reward. I find that people are much more forthcoming if they can profit from it. Greed is a fact of life."

"Rick, I have what may be a better idea," said Barbara. "Why don't we use the Internet. Everybody and his brother is on Facebook or some other social network, or either posts to or reads a blog. I can tell all the people that I friended on Facebook, they in turn can tell all the people they friended, and so on and so forth. I bet we can cover half the globe before it's all said and done. And we can do it instantaneously. We won't have to wait for the news to come on television. I remember when that shooting happened at Fort Hood down in Texas. A friend of mine had a husband who happened to be on the post that day. Even before the story hit the "breaking news," all of us already knew that her husband was all right because she posted it on Facebook. It stands to reason that the men who took Goldie know that her family is looking for her by now, but they don't know that their identities are known. If we get the word out this way, there may be less of a chance that they will hurt her. We can still offer a reward."

"You know, Barbara, you may be on to something," said Rick. "Let's try it your way. Why don't you sit down and compose the message right now."

Barbara sat down at her computer keyboard and began to type.

> My best friend in the world, Marigold Robbins is missing. Those of you who are our mutual friends already are aware of this. Goldie (my nickname for her) has not been seen since about four o'clock this past Friday afternoon. We do not know if she left her home voluntarily or if she was forcibly taken. We have not been approached with any ransom demands. We have consulted with the police department and have filed a missing persons report. I am appealing to all my friends in the network to help us to find Marigold. You can do this by passing this message along to all your friends and asking them to do the same. This way, our appeal can go out to people across the nation via the Internet, thus creating sort of an 'Amber alert' for Goldie. Her daughter and I are offering a reward of one thousand dollars to anyone with information leading to the whereabouts of her mother and my friend. We know that all our friends will not be concerned with a reward, but there may be others out there—even a stranger perhaps—that may know something and will come forward with the information. I am writing a description of Marigold for those people who don't know her. She is a light-skinned African-American. She is sixty-six years of age, although she looks more like fifty. She is five feet seven inches tall and weighs approximately 170 pounds. She has short, dark brown hair, which is streaked with blond. Her eyes are also dark brown, but she may be wearing hazel-colored contact lenses. She has no scars, moles, or other distinguishing features on her face. I am posting a recent photo of Marigold. If anyone has seen

her, please notify me via e-mail (Iwearpurple2@hotmail.com) or the police department (g-ross@pol.org). Thanks for your help to all my friends and all their friends out there in cyberspace.

Barb

Rick, Gregg, and Maryann all read over the message and agreed that Barbara should go ahead and transmit it, which she did. Within a few minutes, some responses came back saying that the message was being passed on to others. The word was out there. The three were hoping that it would soon yield some positive results.

Rick cautioned her about some of the kooks out there who sometimes responded to messages like these. "Barbara, if anyone sends you an e-mail that you believe is legitimate, please forward it to Gregg's computer at the station. In fact, forward anything you get. We've got to get back. We have a few irons in the fire regarding our suspects."

"I've got a pot roast in the oven," said Barbara. "And it should be ready in about twenty minutes. Why don't the two of you stay and sit down and have a good meal? I bet neither of you stopped for lunch today, did you?"

Rick smiled a guilty smile. "Now that you mention it, I think I remember having a bagel with some cream cheese way early this morning, or was that yesterday morning. I really can't remember. We appreciate the offer, but we can't afford to slow down now that we're making some progress. I'll take a rain check on that home-cooked meal, though. I usually have microwave dinners."

After the men left, Barbara noticed that a few more e-mails had come through, most of them expressing their hopes that Marigold would be home soon; none of them contained anything significant, but as Rick had asked, Barbara forwarded them all to Gregg's computer.

CHAPTER 29

Marigold heard the door to the suite click open, and Shelton appeared at the door to the bedroom. He was carrying a tray that contained a teapot and two cups. "Hello, my sweet. I hope you weren't frightened at that little power failure we had. It happens quite a bit when we have thunderstorms. We're at somewhat of a high elevation here, so lightning seems to reach the ground quicker. We have redundancy, though, in the form of backup generators, so the blackouts never last for very long. It's time for you to take the next step toward making history, my dear Marigold, and it will be much, much better for you to be asleep for the journey. So, you and I are going to enjoy a cup of tea together. Yours is spiked with a sedative, so you'll soon begin to feel a bit drowsy. I'm am going to insist that you drink it all down like a good girl, none of that foolishness you tried before to avoid ingesting the medications I brought you. That was very naughty, and it made me very angry. But I forgive you, because you are going to make up for all of that." He kissed her on the lips and handed her the cup of tea. He watched as she sipped it as slowly as she could. See could see him growing impatient. "Don't take all day, Marigold, everything is in place and waiting for you."

About five minutes after she finished the cup of tea, Marigold was unconscious. Shelton went to the door of suite and brought in a hospital gurney. He lifted Marigold from the chair she had been sitting in and gently placed her on the gurney; he then secured her arms and legs with soft restraints and wheeled her out of the room and down to the elevator. He got off on the second floor and wheeled the gurney to the end of the hall and unlocked and entered a door marked Authorized Personnel Only. It was his personal and secret operating room. Travis was already gowned and masked; the mask being mostly because Goldie had never seen his face, and he intended to keep it that way. He placed a blood pressure cuff around her arm, attached a pulse ox device to one of her fingers to monitor the oxygen saturation level of her blood, and attached some leads to her body to monitor her heart rate and rhythm as well. All these devices were hooked up to a monitor with readouts for each function. He took off the gloves he was wearing, washed his hands again, and pulled on a fresh pair of gloves so that he could be as sterile as possible. He was, after all, about to inject a foreign substance into a human brain. He wanted to avoid introducing bacteria as well. He held his breath as Shelton pulled on a pair of latex gloves and picked up the hypodermic needle. He held it up to the light for a moment, as if he was inspecting the contents. Apparently satisfied, he handed the syringe to Travis and stepped back away from the table. Travis cleaned Goldie's skin behind her right ear and pushed the needle in until he reached the exact depth he wanted to achieve; he then depressed the plunger and deposited the fake elixir into Goldie's brain, stinging her with the "bee" for the second time since she had been brought here. He was watching Shelton as Shelton watched the readouts on the monitor that was recording Goldie's heart rate, blood pressure, and oxygen saturation. Shelton's eyes narrowed slightly as he observed only minor changes in some of the numbers, changes that were normal variations. This had never happened before. Even Marigold's first small dose had caused a spike in her blood pressure. He was tremendously pleased that the formula seemed not to be having the usual adverse effect. He knew that Marigold would sleep through the night with no problem; he had given her a strong dose of the sedative. Tomorrow, Travis would double the amount of the elixir, and Marigold would begin to exhibit measurable and documentable signs that the aging process was slowing down, and possibly increased sexual cravings like the lab rats had experienced. He could feel himself becoming excited as he thought about how he would experiment with that particular reaction. He watched the monitor for another forty-five minutes until he was certain that nothing unusual or unexpected was going to happen. He wheeled Marigold back to her room, undressed her, and deposited *her between the silk sheets of her prison bed. When she woke up the next morning, Marigold would be unaware that her life, at least for another day, might have been spared by something as ordinary as a thunderstorm in the Ozarks.*

CHAPTER 30

Gregg remained at his desk long past the time when he was supposed to go off duty; he'd stay all night if he had to. He was reading over all the e-mails Barbara was forwarding and reviewing notes of the investigation to see if he could find something, anything, that they might have missed that was a clue that could help them turn the corner in this case. So far, nothing had popped out. When the phone rang, Rick picked it up. It was Nathaniel Weems, one of the forensics technicians that had processed the scene of the accident that killed Charlie Evans, the maintenance guy.

"Hey, Rick, you know that BMW was equipped with a GPS locator that keeps a log of the trips that were entered into it. We're pulling the information off it now, so we'll be able to tell you soon where the car has been. As for cause of death for Charlie Evans, the medical examiner says that his blood alcohol level was through the roof, and that's most likely the reason he went off the road. He wasn't wearing a seat belt, and his head hit the windshield so hard that it broke his nose and drove a splinter of bone up into his brain. What a way to go, huh. There were lots of fingerprints in the vehicle. We found Charlie's prints, of course, and there are a few sets of unidentified prints, some of which probably belong to your missing woman, but we can't verify because her prints are not in any of our databases. One of the prints matches your coffee cup guy, which of course matches that cold case hit from Chicago. Another set of prints is a match for one Travis Barnwell. Barnwell was in the system because he had a sheet from a while back. He was convicted of larceny by deception, for which he got probation. Nothing shows up since then. As soon as we get that trip log information, I'll call you back. Likewise, if we get anything else significant."

"Gregg, we might have just caught a break," said Rick. "There's a trip log in the BMW, and the forensic techs are pulling the information off it right now. The log will tell you where that BMW has been, and it may be able to lead us to the black SUV. Shelton changed vehicles somewhere, and I'll bet he didn't take a taxi to do it."

Gregg didn't answer because he was distracted by one of the e-mails Barbara had forwarded. "Hey, Rick, check this out," he said as he turned the monitor around so that Rick could read the message. "What do you think this means? Do you think we should take it seriously? It's another connection to Missouri, to Marigold's first e-mail. And remember Travis Mitchell's forwarding address? Did we ever track down the post office box to a specific location?"

Rick read the strange message:

> Barbara, this is Marva in Missouri. I know it's hard to realize that a loved one may have become mentally incapacitated, but it does no good to try to ease your guilt by making others believe that a loved one just disappeared rather than acknowledge that you had them institutionalized for their own good. I know that you know exactly where your mother is. If I were you, I would check on the status of my own mental health.

"Gregg, forward this to Harold," said Rick. "This may be from one of those nutcases we knew would be coming out of the woodwork, but for some reason, I don't think so. This may be somebody who's seen Mrs. Robbins. Tell him we need the IP address *stat*."

Five minutes later Harold called back. "Hey, Rick, I've traced the e-mail to a Starbucks coffee located in a service plaza off US 65 in Missouri. You can call the state patrol guys up there to have them check the place out, but it's my opinion that it would be an exercise in futility. You see, anyone in the nearby vicinity can hijack a Wi-Fi signal and use it. Whoever sent that e-mail may have never even been in the Starbucks. If the person was physically there, he or she is probably gone by now. The e-mail was sent twenty minutes ago. I know it's not what you were hoping to hear, but it does tell you something."

"Yeah, thanks, Harold," said Rick. "You done good, as usual, buddy."

Barbara called Gregg just as Rick was hanging up the phone. Rick could tell from Gregg's side of the conversation that she was asking him about that strange e-mail. "Yes, Mom, we were able to trace it back to the source. It was sent from a Starbucks somewhere out on highway US 65 in Missouri, but that doesn't tell us a whole lot according to our computer guy. No, Mom, that won't do any good. The person didn't even have to be in the Starbucks to send the message. They could have just hijacked a Wi-Fi signal. I know you don't understand, but take my word for it. Yes, we're putting in a call to the authorities there, but I would bet anything that whoever sent that message is long gone by now. I know, Mom, but you're going to have to try to be patient. Believe me, we are making progress. Yes, I love you too. Keep forwarding those e-mails. Bye, Mom."

CHAPTER

31

Twenty minutes earlier, Marva Weiss was on her way home from work and had stopped at a Starbucks in a small strip mall along the highway to pick up a latte and relax for a few minutes. She'd had a stressful day at work. She was a psychiatric social worker, and she was tired of listening to and trying to sort out other people's neuroses. She unpacked her laptop computer and hooked it up to the Wi-Fi connection provided by Starbucks for its customers, thinking that she might as well log on to her Facebook account while she was enjoying the coffee. She missed her friends back home, and she was comforted by keeping in touch with them via the Internet. She thought at first that her eyes were deceiving her when a picture of Marigold with its accompanying message popped up on her monitor. Marva knew, though, that she was not mistaken; this was the same woman she had seen in the luxury suite at that place where Shelton worked, the one he said was a paranoid schizophrenic. She wondered if the message was an elaborate joke. Shelton had told her the woman's family had her committed for treatment because she had tried suicide several times. He told her he couldn't break confidentiality by telling her the patient's real name but said that her family was rich and influential and wanted to keep the commitment a secret and out of the media. She thought back to the morning Shelton had asked her to go into the woman's suite and make sure she ate a healthy breakfast prior to receiving a treatment later that same day. They were lying in his bed after his ministrations had awakened her, and they ended up in a vigorous, almost violent, session of lovemaking. "Marva, my sweet, I have to leave for a few hours for a mandatory meeting with some very important business associates. You know how important my work is to me, and these people provide funding for some of my research. A helicopter is picking me up in one hour. I need you to help me out with one of my special patients. She was very agitated last night and caused herself to regurgitate her evening meal. It is crucially important that she eat this morning. I have written out the menu for you, and you must see to it that she eats everything. You are the only here that I can trust with this task." Then he kissed her on the lips, the breasts, and in much more intimate places until she cried out in pleasure. She loved Shelton, and she had wanted to do whatever he wanted her to do—just to please him. She had trusted him completely. Now, reading that message, she started to wonder if she had been wrong about the handsome, charismatic, doctor.

Marva couldn't force herself to navigate away from the page she was looking at; in the posted picture, Marigold looked healthy and happy. She was conflicted, and question after question went through her mind. What if this wasn't a joke? What if that woman, Marigold Robbins, was really in trouble? What if she was wrong about Shelton? She really didn't know a lot about him, only that she had gone to bed with him after her first date with him three months ago. She remembered that she had felt mesmerized, entranced somehow, and that she couldn't wait to have sex with him. She had never had quite such an intense reaction to a man before. At twenty-eight years of age and unmarried, Marva's sexual encounters were few and far between, and she thought that was the reason she had felt such lust—that's the only word she could use to describe it—for Shelton. She just couldn't allow herself to believe that he could be a kidnapper. She didn't know what she should do. She didn't want to betray Shelton, but on the other hand, she didn't want any harm to come to that woman either. She decided to send a reply as a test. She would see what kind of a response came back and from whom: this Barbara person or the police. She would never be comfortable in Shelton's presence if she didn't find out. She typed out a message and hit Send.

CHAPTER 32

"Your mother is really stressed out, isn't she?" commented Rick after Gregg got off the phone with Barbara. "I'm thinking that this e-mail stuff is making it worse for her."

"Yeah, it probably is, but we've committed to it now, and we've just got to see it through. I think we should respond to that message from Marva. If she's really seen Marigold and knows where she is, maybe we can convince her that the police really are trying to find her, or if she's using that message as a ruse to get more of a reward, then I think we should get her to believe that it's worthwhile to tell us what she knows. If she does reply, her next message may make it clear to us whether or not she is a nutcase, or she may make it possible for us to hone in on a location. In any case, I think it's worth a try."

"I think that's a good idea," said Rick. "If we transmit it from your computer, and Marva knows how to trace an IP address, she will know that it came from the police station. If she's legit, this may be a good chance to get more information. Let's do it."

Gregg sat down at the computer keyboard and begin to type:

> To Marva in Missouri. If you have seen Marigold, then it is critically important that you contact us by replying to our message at the e-mail address contained herein. Marigold Robbins is not—I repeat—is not mentally incapacitated. We believe that she was taken from her home by a person

or persons unknown, and is being held against her will for purposes which may place her life in jeopardy. If you have any information as to her whereabouts, we urge you to contact us immediately. You will be entitled to the one-thousand-dollar reward once Marigold has been safely returned to her home and family.

Gregg Ross
Albemarle County Police Department.

After Gregg sent the message, they called Harold and gave him the scenario, and he had them set Gregg's computer up to forward any reply directly to him so he could get to work on it immediately. Then they sat down and waited, but the computer remained silent.

Rick got up to pour himself a cup of stale coffee from the office coffeemaker. He had been at it since he got out of bed at six o'clock Monday morning, and he was not as young and dynamic as he used to be. He hoped the caffeine would reenergize him because he had the feeling it was going to be a long night. The coffee was hot, but it had been sitting so long that it was bitter; it certainly lived up the reputation that all coffee brewed in police stations was some version of mud.

He had just returned to his desk when Nathaniel Weems walked into the room and handed him a printout; it was the GPS trip log for the BMW. Together, he and Gregg read through the entries. Rick logged on to the Internet, looked up some information, which he jotted down in his notebook, then the two men picked up their jackets and headed for the door. On the way out, Gregg stuck his head in the commander's office and told him where they were headed. A backup team was ordered to follow them in case they located the suspects. The location from the trip log that caught their attention was a private heliport located about thirty minutes out in Crozet. The trip log had recorded several trips to the heliport in the BMW. Their thinking was that if Marigold had been abducted and taken out of the state, what better way to do it than by helicopter.

On the way to the facility, Rick called the number of the contact person for the heliport that he had found on the Internet. The call went directly to voice mail, which could be a problem if no one was on site to let them have access. This was a likely possibility since it was already after dark. Rick was thinking now that they probably should have waited to try to get a search warrant.

There was a guard booth at the entrance to the airstrip, and it was still manned even at this time of day. They could see three helicopters sitting idle on the field. Two large warehouse-like buildings loomed in the background. Rick and Gregg identified themselves, showed their badges, and Rick said to the security guard, "We're investigating the disappearance of a woman who may have been brought here and taken aboard one of your helicopters. This would have been on Friday, say around five o'clock in the afternoon. Were you on duty at that time, Frank? That's your name, right, that's what it says on your name tag."

"Yeah, I'm Frank, and yeah, I was on duty Friday, and no, I didn't see no woman getting in a helicopter. So, if you wanna ask me anything else, ask it fast, because I'm off duty in five minutes, and I don't get paid no overtime to stand around and jaw with the po-lice."

Rick was tired, and he lost his patience immediately. "Frank, you'd better lose the attitude, because this is serious. The woman we're asking about was kidnapped, and if you know something about it, you'd better tell us or you may find yourself going down a road you don't want to travel. Now, let's try this again, and I'll ask it really simple like this time in case you have trouble understanding. Did you see anyone go past your guard booth onto the grounds at around five o'clock Friday afternoon?"

"Well, that's not what you asked me the first time," whined Frank. "How can I answer some question you didn't even ask? The boss called me at four and told me a guy in a black van was coming in at five and that he would show me a permit and I was to let him on the property. I think I seen that van before, or one like it. I did exactly what the boss said to do. I didn't see no woman get on no helicopter like I told you the first time."

"Frank, did you come out of your mother's womb retarded, or did you get dropped on your head?" said Rick. "Now, where did that van go after it went through the gate, and did a helicopter take off after that?"

"Why you got to dis me like that, man. Well, I can't rightly say, I mean, I don't know," said Frank. "Them helicopters come and go all the time, and it ain't part of my job to keep track of 'em. One might've took off after the van drove in. I'm not sure because I had to go over to the facilities, you know, the johnnie over there. I was in there quite a long time, you know. I musta ate too much chili for lunch—it was extra hot and peppery. When I came back out, I didn't see the van no more."

"Frank did you even learn your ABCs and how to count when you were in school? There can't be that many helicopters parked out here at any given time. I only see three right now. You trying to tell me that you can't even count high enough to tell when one is missing?"

"You don't have no cause to go insulting me like that. Can I go now? I'm off duty. I need to put the chain across the gate."

"Afraid not, Frank," said Rick. "We need to see what's in those buildings out there. You got keys."

"Yeah, but I don't think I'm supposed to let you do that. I need to call up my boss. I don't wanna lose my job." He pulled out a cell phone and dialed a number. When someone picked up on the other end, he said "I got a coupla po-lice out here saying they got to look in the buildings. Am I supposed to let them in? They was asking did anybody come in the gate Friday in the evening, and something about some woman they think took a helicopter ride on Friday. I told them about the guy you told me to let in, and I told them I didn't see no woman take no ride on Friday, but they say they gotta look anyway. Do I have to wait? It's coming up on my off-duty time now. Well, can I get overtime for it then? Okay, boss, I got you." He ended the call and turned to the police. "The boss says to wait right here. He's coming, and he'll be here in fifteen minutes. I got to wait till he gets here. I'm gonna miss the first part of the game."

"I'm sure you'll get over it Frank," said Rick. "There'll always be another game on tomorrow, and you may not have to watch it from behind bars."

Rick took Gregg aside. "If the boss gets here and he's got something to hide, he may insist on a warrant before we can look around. If we can't get a warrant, then he'll have time to get rid of anything incriminating. I don't want to take that chance. I think we need to talk that genius in the guard booth into giving us the keys so we can have a peek before the boss gets here."

"I say we go for it," said Gregg. "But let me call the commander and at least ask him to get started on a search warrant. If we find anything in the buildings, we will need forensic techs to get out here and process the evidence on a fast-track-basis." Gregg got on his cell phone, dialed his commander, and explained the situation. He left out the part about him and Rick deciding to go in immediately. He closed his cell phone and said, "Okay, Rick, let's do it."

Rick walked back over to the guard booth. "Hey Frank, since the boss is on his way to let us in, I don't see the harm in you taking off. That way you won't have to miss the game. We'll hold onto the keys and explain to the boss that we told you to go. I'm sure it'll be all right. After all, we are the po-lice," laughed Rick.

Frank was anxious to leave; he wasn't really going to watch a game on TV. He was meeting up with a girl he met in a strip club a few nights before. She had promised to sleep with him if he was nice to her. He knew that meant it would cost him money. He hadn't slept with anybody in a long time, and he was very excited. His body was reacting just thinking about Patty with her luscious body. He didn't give a second thought to handing over the keys. He headed to his pickup truck and peeled rubber out of there.

Gregg and Rick walked over to the first building and unlocked the door. The building was a hangar; there were two helicopters inside. They looked old and in disuse. They walked over to the second building, unlocked it, and pulled up the rolling garage doors. Inside, sitting side by side, were two black SUV's, one a 2009 Chrysler Aspen, the other an older SUV with a parking sticker and a fountain logo still attached on the back window. Gregg was just about to use his cell phone to report what they had found to the commander and to call for a forensic tech team to process the vehicles when a voice behind them snarled, "What the hell are you two doing in here? This is private property. You had no right to come in here before I got here. I told that idiot Frank to tell you to wait. Unless you can show me a warrant, you need to get out right now."

"Are you the owner of this heliport?" asked Rick.

"Yes, I am, I'm Nathan Rogers, and you don't have a warrant, do you? I didn't think so. I'm going to sue you and your department for trespassing." He pulled out his cell phone. "I'm calling my lawyer right now."

"Yeah, Nathan, you do that," said Rick. "You're going to need a lawyer, my man, because these two vehicles you are housing in this building may just make you an accomplice to a kidnapping where the victim was transported across state lines. That's a federal offense. How would you like to spend say, the next twenty years or so of your life in prison? How does that sound, Nathan? You do have an alternative. You can cooperate with us, tell us what we want to know, and maybe convince us that you had nothing to do with the kidnapping of one Marigold Robbins, a mother, grandmother and law-abiding citizen of the state of Virginia. To tell you the truth, Nathan, we didn't need a warrant to get into this building. We had the keys, which were given to us voluntarily by your agent, the security guard."

Gregg's cell phone rang; it was his commander telling him that the search warrant was on the way.

Rick continued to push Nathan. "The search warrant is on its way, Nathan. If you need to tell us something, now is the time, my man. Once we find incriminating evidence against you, we will arrest you and throw your butt in jail. Do not pass Go, do not collect two million dollars."

"Look, Detective whatever your name is," said Nathan. "All I did was rent storage space to a client over the phone. I never even saw him, and I just called Frank—by the way he's fired as of right now—to tell him when the guy showed to let him on the property. I don't know about him taking a helicopter. I only own the property and the buildings. I rent space to the guy that owns the helicopters."

He took out a pen and paper and wrote down a name and phone number. "Talk to this guy about that."

Gregg led Nathan over to a desk in the corner of the room and told him to have a seat in one of the two chairs; Rick punched in the number Nathan had given. The call went to voice mail, just as expected. He decided to wait for the forensics techs to get here and go over the cars before he tried to track down the helicopter operator. He could still hear that clock ticking in his head.

CHAPTER

33

Marva Weiss opened her laptop the minute she got home; sure enough, there was a reply to her message, with instructions for her to reply back—directly to the Albemarle County Police Department in Virginia. "Oh, my God," she said out loud. "Shelton, who are you and what have you done?" Marva was frightened, both of Shelton and of the implications of that e-mail message. He had made her an unwitting part of a criminal conspiracy. She wondered if it meant that she could go to jail too. And that message had said they thought Marigold Robbins's life was in danger. Did that mean hers might be too? Why did Shelton kidnap that woman and bring her here? The e-mail said no ransom demands had been made, so he didn't take her for money. She was reasonably certain he didn't take her for sex; the woman was in her sixties, for God's sake. Shelton might call her at any minute and tell her to come to that place where he both worked and lived. He told her it was a combination mental health hospital and luxury rehab facility for the rich and famous. The complex was isolated, high up in the mountains. It consisted of five different buildings; Marva had been inside only one. Shelton's living quarters were in the same building where she saw Marigold. She hated driving to it, especially at night, but, until now, she was so in heat whenever she heard Shelton's voice that she jumped at his every beck and call. She pondered what she should do. If she sent another e-mail, the cops might trace it back to her computer and come arrest her. She could tell them what she had seen, but she couldn't prove a thing. She closed the laptop without sending another message.

CHAPTER 34

The forensics technicians arrived at the heliport thirty minutes after Gregg called them. They immediately began to go over the two vehicles with a fine-tooth comb. As expected, they found several sets of fingerprints on the vehicles. In the older SUV, they found prints matching prints in the BMW; those belonging to Travis, those presumably belonging to Shelton because they matched the ones on the coffee container and the cold case hit. In the back of the van, on a blanket, they found some short, dark-brown strands of hair. The techs looked at the strands under one of the microscopes that was part of the equipment in their crime scene vehicle; the strands were streaked with a blond dye. They also found a single hazel-tinted contact lens. Rick took these two things as conclusive evidence that Marigold Robbins had been in the back of that SUV. In the newer model SUV, the 2009 Chrysler Aspen, they got a hit on Travis's prints, plus a number of unidentified ones.

While the techs were processing the vehicles, Rick continued to try to get hold of the helicopter operator, calling both home and cell phones. He left voice mail messages each time he called. After the fifth time, a woman called him back.

"Hello, is this Detective Rick Williams?" When Rick answered in the affirmative, the woman continued, "I'm Tamika Copland, and I see from the many voice mail messages that you have been trying to reach my husband, Andrew. May I ask what this is about?"

"Mrs. Copland, I'm sorry to disturb you, but it is vitally important that I speak with your husband on a police matter."

"Detective, has Andrew done something wrong? If he has, please tell me. I have a right to know."

"Ma'am, at this point, we're not saying that Mr. Copland has done anything wrong, but we need to ask him some questions about an ongoing investigation. Can you tell me where we can reach him?"

"Well, he's out of town at the moment. He went to a pilot's convention on the West Coast, but I expect him back tonight. His flight is supposed to get in at ten o'clock. I'm supposed to pick him up at the airport."

"Mrs. Copland," said Rick, "is there any way you can get in touch with him right now? We'd rather talk to him sooner than later. Like I said before, it's extremely urgent."

"You can try his cell phone. I can give you the number, but I've been trying to call him myself, and he doesn't answer. If he's in the air, his phone is turned off. Sometimes he turns it off anyway, I think just to get a break from so many people calling him all the time."

"I've already tried his cell number several times, and he didn't answer for me either, so maybe it is turned off. Mrs. Copland, do you assist him in running the helicopter business? Would you know if he had a flight scheduled this past Friday evening, and if so, where did he go and who were his passengers?"

"Detective, we are an old-fashioned household. I am a housewife and a stay-at-home mom. My husband is the breadwinner. I take care of our home and care for the children. Andrew pays all the bills and never involves me in any aspect of his business. I don't even know the first thing about helicopters and have never been in one myself because I have a fear of flying. Andrew left home very early Friday morning, and I didn't see him again until around one o'clock on Saturday, but that is not unusual. Sometimes he even flies overnighters."

"Mrs. Copland, you've been very cooperative, and I thank you," said Rick. "If you do hear from your husband, please tell him that he needs to call me immediately. You have the number. If I don't hear from him by the time his plane is due to arrive, please tell him to expect us to meet him at the airport."

"All right, if I hear from Andrew before his plane lands, I'll be sure to give him your message, Detective Williams. Good-bye."

Rick relayed the conversation to Gregg. He looked at his watch. It was now eight o'clock. They had two hours before Andrew Copland was due to land at Albemarle Airport. He hoped the man would call before then.

CHAPTER
35

Shelton was enraged. He's just found out that Travis, the snake, had tricked him. He had gone back to the lab to look at the blood that had been drawn after Marigold's injection. He spent fifteen minutes peering at the slides under the microscope. He didn't see even one of the markers that were supposed to be there. Just to make sure that he wasn't mistaken, he went to Marigold's bedroom and drew another vial of blood. Maybe he just had not waited long enough after the injection to see the markers he was looking for. This latest blood sample looked as the same as the others. He went to Travis's sleeping quarters and viciously yanked the bedcovers off the sleeping man and shouted at him, "Get up. Did you really think you could get away with it, Travis? What kind of fool do you take me for? You didn't give Marigold the elixir. You'd better have a damn good explanation why you did not. I could kill you right now with my bare hands. I will not allow a sniveling coward like you ruin my research and destroy my life's work."

"Shelton, listen to me," said Travis. "I really didn't try to circumvent your procedure. I had an accident with the buffering agent. When the lights went out, I knocked a vial to the floor. You said I had to be ready by six o'clock, and I knew you'd be livid just like you are now if I told you what happened, so I just gave her a placebo to give me time to percolate more buffer. You know I couldn't inject her with the raw elixir, it would've burned a hole in her brain. I've got more of the agent ready now. We can repeat the procedure in the morning. No real harm has been done. It was an accident—I swear it was."

"You don't understand, do you, you idiot?" shouted Shelton. "Everything has been planned according to a strict protocol. Everything has been timed to the day. Marigold's body has been prepped to receive the injections on a specific timetable. Now you have caused a delay. You may have ruined everything."

"Shelton, try to calm down. Nothing has been ruined. Remember that I am as familiar with your protocol as you are. I told you that you were rushing things. Marigold didn't even get the prerequisite doses of the prep because you were rushing things. Think about it, that accident might have saved your procedure. We can go ahead and give her some more prep tonight and repeat the injection of the elixir in the morning. You know I'm right."

"She's still out from the sedative I gave her, Travis. Just how do you propose I give her more prep, pour it down her throat while she's unconscious?

"I can administer it to her intravenously, Shelton. You can prepare it yourself, or you can watch me get it ready if you don't trust me. I'm not trying to deceive you. Don't you think I want you to succeed with this? I want to get out of this godforsaken place and go someplace warm where I don't have to hide from the authorities."

"Get the IV equipment ready and meet me in Marigold's room. I'll give you twenty minutes. If you're not there by then, I will go to my room and get my gun and put it in your ear and pull the trigger. If you think I'm not serious, just be late."

Travis breathed a sigh of relief that he was still alive. Shelton was definitely psychotic. He quickly threw on some clothes and ran down to the lab and grabbed the IV setup and some latex gloves. He took the elevator to Marigold's room. It took him less than fifteen minutes. Shelton was waiting with the jar of milky liquid. Travis set up the IV and timed the drip so that the solution would flow into her system in thirty minutes. Marigold stirred briefly when he was inserting the needle for the IV site, but she did not come fully awake. Travis wondered if the woman was dreaming, and if so, was it a nightmare, like the one he was experiencing? Shelton watched him like a hawk the whole time. He needed haven't worried. Travis was sufficiently terrified and had no intention of doing anything other than what Shelton told him to do. He motioned to a chair *beside the bed. Travis sat down and waited. After the IV was finished, he unhooked the apparatus and looked to Shelton for further direction.*

"What time is it now, Travis?" asked Shelton. Travis looked at his watch, a fake Rolex. *He hadn't wanted to spend money on a real one; he preferred to waste his funds on women and gambling.* "It's eight o'clock."

"Travis, I am going to give you some instructions. Listen very carefully. You are to return to the lab right now and prepare another injection with a full-strength dosage of the elixir. Make sure that you do not have another accident if you value your life. At precisely 2:00 a.m.—and remember that I said precisely—you will return to this room with a gurney. You will check Marigold's vitals. You will then place her back under anesthesia and wheel her back down to the operating room, where you will inject her with the elixir, full-strength, all of it. I see that you are about to open your mouth to protest, but it will do you no good to argue that her body needs until the morning to metabolize the prep. It is due to your carelessness that we find ourselves in this hurry-up mode. By morning, I intend to know whether my formula is viable. You may leave now. I'm going to stay here with my sweet Marigold until you return at 2:00 a.m.. You see, I really do care about her."

Travis almost ran from the suite. He hurried to the lab and began his preparations. In his mind's eye, the only thing he could see clearly was a huge gun being inserted in his ear and a loud boom (the last sound he would ever hear) as the trigger was pulled. He thought about making a run for it, but even if he could steal one of the vehicles sitting in the parking lot, he knew it was doubtful he could find his way off the mountain in the dark. He was trapped. He had no choice but to do what that madman Shelton wanted him to do. He also knew that it was unlikely that the Robbins woman would survive.

While waiting in Marigold's room, Shelton smiled inwardly as he thought about the plans he had formulated for her last infusion of the elixir, plans he had no intention of sharing with Travis until the last minute. That way he wouldn't have to listen to the man's cowardly protestations. Shelton had come to the conclusion that the material needed to be introduced directly into the hippocampus of Marigold's brain. He believed that the antiaging effect would begin immediately and dramatically. There was one drawback. The procedure would necessitate cutting into Marigold's outer brain and opening a window into the temporal lobe to reach the hippocampus. Neither he nor Travis were surgeons—hell, he wasn't even a doctor, and Travis was a poor excuse for one. Shelton had contacted a neurosurgeon named Lionel Beckton. Beckton was a first-class neurosurgeon, but like Travis, he had expensive appetites. Lionel's happened to be for certain illegal substances, the overindulgence of which had ultimately cost him his license to practice medicine and caused his wife to divorce him. In addition to needing cash for his habits, Lionel now had to dish out child support for his two adolescent children. He jumped at the chance to get the $500,000 that Shelton was going to pay him for performing what to him was a simple surgery. No questions asked. Shelton dialed the man's number on his cell phone and gave him directions to the facility and told him precisely when to arrive. Shelton ended the conversation with a warning, "Lionel, you understand that you will never talk about the surgery to anyone, you will never try to come back to me for more money, and you will develop amnesia about what you do and who you see. After you leave here, I will never hear from you again. If I do, it will be the worst and last mistake you make in this life. Are we clear?"

Lionel answered in the affirmative, "Of course, Shelton, you know that I wouldn't screw with you."

"And one last thing," snarled Shelton, just before he clicked off, "do not show up here high with whatever you sniff up your nose or shoot into your veins, or you will be very, very sorry."

CHAPTER 36

At nine thirty, Rick and Gregg had just about given up hope that Andrew Copland was going to call before his plane got in at ten o'clock. When his cell phone rang, Rick answered it immediately thinking that at last the helicopter operator was on the line.

"Hello, this Rick Williams," he said.

"Hello, yourself, and I already know who you are," said Harold, the computer tech. "I take it you were expecting somebody else."

"Yeah, Harold, I was kind of hoping, but do you have something for me?"

"I've got another e-mail from Marva in Missouri. It was received ten minutes ago. If you're ready, I'll forward it to your phone."

"Go ahead and send it, Harold," said Rick.

> To the police in Albemarle County. I am not involved in any way with any kidnapping, but I have seen Marigold Robbins. She is being held on the fourth floor at a mental hospital and rehab facility called Center for Rejuvenation. It's up in the Ozark mountains. She seemed all right when I saw her, but I had been led to believe she was a paranoid schizophrenic. I do not want a reward. I do not know what is being done to Marigold Robbins, but on Sunday, she was being prepared for some kind of procedure. I will not name the

person that I think is holding her because I don't want to accuse anyone when I have no proof. I know this individual personally, and now I am afraid for my own safety. Please hurry.

Harold came back on the line. "Rick, I already have a location for you for that place. The e-mail is right. It's high up in the Ozarks. I briefed your commander, and he got in touch with the authorities out there. They say that it's really off the beaten path and hard to reach in the dark. They say they thought the place was closed down. They want to wait until morning light to drive up there. They're a small police force and don't have a helicopter. The commander explained that something sinister is going on, and that the morning might be too late, but they're adamant that it's too dangerous a drive in the dark. My satellite image shows a complex consisting of five buildings. One building is five stories tall, the others are one to two stories. There's helicopter pad on the roof of one of the buildings. That's an option if you guys want to try to get there tonight. There's no police copter available right now, but if that guy you're waiting for shows up, maybe you can hitch a ride on one of his copters. If he flew Marigold and the perps up there, he already knows where the place is, and he has an incentive to cooperate if it's made clear to him what kind of jam he could be in. Is it true that you guys can put Marigold in that black SUV?"

"Yeah, we got some strands of hair that are consistent with Marigold's, and we found a hazel-colored contact lens. Her friend and her daughter said she sometimes wore some that color. And there were some prints in there that matched prints we pulled out of the BMW. I think we've got enough to bring those guys in. Thanks, Harold, I'll keep you posted."

Gregg called Barbara and told her that "Marva from Missouri" had e-mailed them again directly to the police station and told them where she thought they could find Marigold. "Mom, she says she saw Marigold on Sunday, and she seemed to be all right. She's being held on the fourth floor of the only high-rise building at the site. The place is somewhere up in the Ozarks. We've contacted the local authorities, but they seem reluctant to get up there tonight. They say it's dangerous traveling by car in the dark. Rick and I are trying to get hold of a helicopter so we can go up their ourselves." He could hear both Barbara and Maryann crying on the other end.

"You be careful son," said Barbara. "And please, please bring Goldie back to us."

Rick and Gregg were waiting along with Mrs. Copland when Andrew Copland's plane landed. As soon as he entered the terminal, Rick and Gregg identified themselves and took him aside to question him while his wife and son retrieved his luggage.

"Mr. Copland," said Rick, "we're investigating the disappearance of a Virginia resident, Mrs. Marigold Robbins. We believe she was abducted on Friday by a man named Shelton Maxwell, who may have been accompanied by a man named Travis Mitchell or Travis Barnwell. Take a look at these photos. Do you know either of these men?"

"Well, yeah, I know both of them, but this one said his name was Marshall, not Maxwell. They're both doctors. They work up at that place in the mountains, you know, that place for rich wackos. I flew them up on Friday night with a nutcase, a woman."

Rick showed the man a smiling photo of Marigold. "Is this the woman, Mr. Copland?" he asked.

"You know, I really couldn't tell because Dr. Marshall told me she had to be sedated for the trip because she was a violent nutcase and he didn't want her causing a disturbance once we were in the air. I never actually got a good look at her. Are you saying those doctors are kidnappers? I can't believe it. They just didn't seem like the type, you know, always wore nice suits and talked all professional. I hope you don't think I had anything to do with a kidnapping. They paid me a bonus for going up there at night. You have to know where you're going, or you could get in real trouble. They got a regular helipad though with proper lights, so I didn't have a problem."

"At this point, we don't have any reason to believe that you participated in the kidnapping, Mr. Copland, but let me ask you a question. You said you're familiar with that facility up in the Ozarks. Does that mean you've flown these two guys up there before?" asked Rick.

"Yeah, they took another woman up there a while back, but this was the first time we've gone at night. Come to think of it, they had that other patient sedated too, and I never got a good look at her either. She was old, though, because I saw a flash of gray hair. The doctors have always called me to fly them back a few days later without the passenger on board."

"Mr. Copland," said Rick, "we believe that Mrs. Robbins's life is in imminent danger, and we need to get up to that facility as fast as possible. We've notified the authorities up there, but they believe it extremely dangerous for them to drive up there in the dark. We've also notified the FBI, and we're hoping they'll go wheels up as soon as they get clearance to do so. We need your help. You're our best bet for getting there fast. Can you use one of your copters to fly us up there right now? You'll be repaid, but if you're worried about fuel, we'll take care of the cost ourselves right now."

"The thing is, Detective," said Copland, "it's going to take at least five hours to get up there. Isn't there some other way to do this? Maybe get a jet into some airport close by and then take a copter from there. You did say that this lady is in immediate danger."

"Look," said Rick, "I'm hoping that the Feds will get there sooner than we can. They have far more resources in far more places, but I don't yet have confirmation from them, and we can't just stand around, wishing and hoping and trying to make arrangements that may or may not pan out. We need to get moving now—are you helping us or not?"

"All right, already," said Copland. "Are you always so quick to get your back up? I was just trying to help. Maybe we can save some time. I have an associate who houses his copters right here at this airport. Let me make a phone call and see if we can use one of his. That way, we won't have to travel back out to the heliport where my copters are parked." He pulled out his cell and made a call as he walked over to his wife and son and told them he wasn't going home with them right now. His wife seemed to be protesting, but Andrew said something that sent her on her way. When he came back, he told Rick and Gregg that his associate had given his okay to use one of his copters. Andrew led the way to the helicopter, a sleek Westland Lynx, touted as being the world's fastest copter. "Good news," he said, as he climbed aboard. "This baby can do over two hundred miles per hour, so I can get you there in a little over three hours." He began his preflight check, motioned Rick and Gregg aboard, and called the tower to get approval of his flight plan before he got underway. Rick and Gregg belted themselves in for the ride. Gregg checked his wristwatch as the copter rotors began to turn. It was 11:00 p.m.

CHAPTER

37

Marva Weiss couldn't get the image of Marigold out of her mind. She wanted to do something to help the woman, but she didn't know what. She hoped that the police had gotten her e-mail and were on the way here to stop Shelton from doing whatever he was planning to do to that poor woman. She was startled when her cell phone rang; the ring tone was "Forever Young," so she knew it was Shelton. He had insisted on having a "special" ring tone just for him. Marva's heart seemed to fly right into her throat, but she did the best she could to calm her breathing and speak in a normal tone of voice when she answered the call.

"Hello, my sweet little dove," he crooned. "I need your loving right now, so please fly to my side so I can spread your little wings and come inside."

"Shelton, you know how I hate driving up the mountain in the dark," she answered, although for some inexplicable reason—despite what she had learned about him—she still felt the stirring of desire in her loins as soon as she heard his voice. What in the world is wrong with me, *she thought?* The man's a criminal, a kidnapper or worse, but I still want him. *"Shelton, why don't we wait until daylight? I'll come to you at first light, and we can make love for hours before it's time for me to start work."*

"Oh, no, Marva, that won't do at all. I have other plans for a few hours from now. I need you urgently, right now, and I have a feeling that your need for me—right now—is just as urgent. Don't make me wait. Be

here in one hour. It would make me very unhappy if I have to come for you." He clicked off his cell phone without waiting for her reply.

Marva was stunned. How could it be that she had never heard the menace in voice before. It was obvious that she had no choice but to go to him. She was terrified, but at the same time she kept remembering how it felt to have him make love to her. She was ashamed that he was right—she wanted him so much right then that she could hardly stand it. She wondered if his reference to "other plans" had something to do with Marigold Robbins. As she was packing a tote, it occurred to her that if she could find the nerve, there might be a way for her to help the woman. The remote control to open Marigold's door was in Shelton's suite. His lovemaking was so vigorous that he often fell asleep after a session. Perhaps she could get hold of the device and get the woman out of there. They could both make a run for it down the mountain, or maybe find someplace to hide. Hopefully, that would give the police time to get there and take care of Shelton. If only she did have the nerve. She had to stop her whole body from trembling at the very thought of defying the man.

Shelton laughed with delight as he thought about how easily he could manipulate the mousy little woman. A few drops of the right liquid had turned her into his sexual slave, who was at his beck and call. He could not quite remember ever being so horny as he waited for Marva. Perhaps his high state of anticipation was because he knew that in a few hours he would realize his greatest dream. That fool Travis was a pessimist, but Shelton knew he would be successful this time. He was going to be rich and famous. After he finished with Marva tonight, he wouldn't need her anymore. The richest and most beautiful women in the world would be his for the taking. He wouldn't have to slip them anything to enhance their libido, like he did for Marva. She'd never know why she always wanted him so much. Maybe he'd market that product too. He suddenly thought of Marigold, his pot of gold. He went up to her suite to see if she was still out. She was restless, moving around, perhaps dreaming. He was sorry that he had never made love to her. Mature women had something so special to offer. He indulged himself for a moment and took the covers off Marigold's bed. He reached under her clothing and caressed her beautiful breasts and stroked her supple hips. He wanted *to go further but restrained himself. After all, he wasn't a pervert. He wanted his partners to be willing participants. He rearranged her clothing, left the room, and returned to his suite to wait for his little dove to fly into his arms. He would make love to Marva until time for him to finish the procedure on Marigold, then he would give her something special to make her sleep. Should the worst happen—as predicted by Travis—then he would see to it that his little dove never made it back down the mountain. The mountains were treacherous; her body would probably never be found. He decided that he needed to make contingency plans for Travis too. The little weasel was becoming a liability. He needed him, though, for the time being, to document the results of the procedures on Marigold. It was his firm belief that she would survive to become living proof of his genius but—just in case—he needed hard clinical data to present to the medical community. The fact that he was committing multiple serious crimes did nothing to mitigate Shelton's elation about the miracle that was about to occur.*

CHAPTER 38

Rick and Gregg had been in the air for two hours when a call was patched through from the FBI to let them know that the bureau had reviewed the elements of the case and were convinced that a kidnapped person had been transported across state lines. A team of field agents were in the air on their way to the facility at the Ozarks. ETA about two hours from now. That would put them there about 3:00 a.m. Strong headwinds had slowed the speed of the Lynx and caused Rick, who was a reluctant flyer at best, to go silent. His face was white and pinched as he fought off spasms of nausea. It would be extremely embarrassing to him to have to use the "barf" bag. Andrew, meanwhile, was using every skill he had as a pilot to push the Lynx to its max; he still hoped to get them there shortly after 2:00 a.m. Gregg hoped they would not be too late.

Back in Virginia, Barbara and Maryann went online with their friends and asked them all to pray that Marigold would be found alive and well and would be returned to them. Word went out to friends of friends, and soon, all over the country, prayers were being sent up to whatever God each person worshipped. Waiting was excruciating.

CHAPTER

39

Marva was terrified of the drive up the dark mountain road; she was more terrified of Shelton. She made it back up to the facility by 10:30 p.m. Shelton was waiting for her in his room, clad only in a robe. He pulled her immediately into his arms and let the robe fall open. She could see and feel his readiness. He smelled of a subtle cologne and, despite her fear, she began to become incredibly turned on. He poured them both a glass of white wine and lay down on the bed and took a tiny sip of his while he watched her take off her street clothes and pick up a sexy negligee. She knew that Shelton loved to watch her don the lingerie and then strip it from her body as part of his ritual of foreplay. Tonight was different. He stood up and suddenly ripped the garment from her hands and directed her to finish her glass of wine while standing naked before him like she was an exhibit on display. Inexplicably, she flushed with embarrassment, even though he had seen her naked on several occasions. She finished the glass of wine and, almost immediately, began to feel a sexual need so urgent that she literally wanted to run over to the bed and impale herself on him. His smile seemed diabolical, almost as if he knew exactly what she was thinking and feeling and suddenly—like a light bulb being turned—she realized that he had put something in the wine. What a fool she had been. No wonder she had been so turned on whenever she was with him. He had been giving her drugs to amp up her libido! And what an effective drug it was; her mind was telling her to flee right now, her body was attracted to him like a moth to a flame. He beckoned with his finger, and like a programmed robot, Marva went to him. He pulled her down on the bed and began to kiss and caress her in ways that drove her to distraction. She forgot about Marigold, she forgot about her fear of this man who was touching her in maddening ways, she forgot about everything except her urgent need for him.

Their lovemaking session went on for what seemed like hours before Marva's senses returned and left her quaking with fear. Shelton was asleep beside her, and Marva slipped out from underneath the covers and waited to see if he would wake up before she moved away from the bed. He didn't stir, so she crept over to the dresser—fortunately, it was on her side of the bed, and Shelton was turned away from it—and silently pulled drawers open to see if she could find the remote device that opened Marigold's door. All the drawers were empty; disappointment settled on her like a brick. Marva tried to think; where would Shelton put the device? He certainly wouldn't hide it from her because he thought he had nothing to fear from her. She thought of a saying, "hiding in plain sight," and she went into the bathroom, closing the door behind her, and saw Shelton's shaving kit laying open on the counter. A smallish device, looking much like a miniature computer mouse, lay inside the pouch.

She grabbed a robe from a hook from behind the door, put it on, and slipped the device into the pocket. Her heart jumped into her throat when she opened the bathroom door and saw Shelton sitting up in bed and looking directly at her.

"Ah, my little dove," he crooned. "I wondered where you had flown. What are you doing, and why are you wearing my robe?" "I ... ah, had to use the bathroom," stammered Marva, hoping he hadn't picked up on how nervous she was. "And I was feeling a little chilly—you know the air-conditioning is turned up a little too high in here."

"Take that robe off and come back to bed, then," said Shelton. "I know exactly how to warm you up." Now that the aphrodisiac drug had worn off, the last thing in the world Marva wanted to do was get back into bed with this man she was so afraid of, but she had no choice. She couldn't let him discover what she was up to. She discarded the robe carefully, letting it drop to the floor by the side of the bed. The thick carpet muffled any thump the small remote device might have made. She realized that she was in trouble; if Shelton didn't go back to sleep, not only couldn't she get out of the room to try to rescue Marigold, she wouldn't be

able to return the device to Shelton's shaving kit. If he planned to use it tonight, as Marva suspected he did, he would know that she had taken it. Her heart was beating so furiously with fright that she had the feeling that Shelton would hear it.

"What is going on with you, my little dove," said Shelton. "You seem nervous. I've got something here to calm you down and get you ready for sweet lovemaking again." He poured her another glass of wine. Marva knew the effect the wine would have on her. "I'm feeling a little dizzy right now, Shelton," she protested. "I'm not used to drinking so much wine. Please, can we just make love. I don't need the wine."

"Oh no, no, I insist that you drink it, my sweet. It will make you feel so much better and so much more ready to fulfill my needs." When Marva began to shake her head, Shelton tilted her head and began to pour the wine down her throat. When she began to choke and sputter, he hesitated only momentarily to allow her to catch her breath and poured every bit of the liquid into her mouth. Instead of feeling the sexual charge she had felt with the first glass of wine, Marva began to feel faint, and the room seemed to recede. Seemingly, from a long way off, she heard Shelton snarl, "You stupid cow." The last thing she saw as she fell into unconsciousness was Shelton picking up the robe she had discarded on the floor, removing the remote device from the pocket, and leaving the room. On his way out, he used a similar remote device to activate an alarm for the door. If Marva gained consciousness before he finished with Marigold and tried to leave the room, an alarm signal would be sent to the device. He had given her enough to keep her out for hours, but he always planned for contingencies.

Minutes after Shelton left the room, Marva Weiss vomited. Fortunately for her, when she passed out, she was lying on her side with her head hanging slightly over the bed, so when she regurgitated, the material did not go into her lungs and cause asphyxiation. Some of the drug had already gotten into her bloodstream, so she didn't wake up immediately but, within thirty minutes, groggily began to become aware of her surroundings. She got off the bed and discovered that her legs were rubbery and didn't seem to work right, so she crawled to where she had discarded her clothing and her purse and found her cell phone. She had decided that even if she did get into trouble, she had to try to help Marigold. The effort to crawl over to her belongings had given her extreme vertigo; the room started to spin, her vision blurred, and she collapsed to the floor, unable to proceed any further.

Shelton was angry, lividly so; he couldn't believe that the woman had tried to thwart his plans. What did she think she was going to do, somehow rescue Marigold? He wondered now what else Marva had done. Had she notified the authorities? He had to move his plans up; he had to finish the procedure so he could get out of there as fast as possible. His plan to have Beckton open a window into Marigold's brain had to be scuttled now. The neurosurgeon wasn't even due to arrive at the facility until the next morning. He looked at his watch. It was 1:30 a.m. He took out his phone and sent a text to Beckton, telling him to abort. He then took the elevator up to Travis's room and rousted him out of bed.

"What the hell ...," began Travis. "What are you doing here? I know the timetable. My alarm is set to go off in forty-five minutes so I can prepare Marigold at two thirty like you said."

"There's been an unexpected development and the timetable has been moved up," said Shelton.

"What kind of development," questioned Travis, suddenly even more apprehensive that he had been.

"That's not you concern," snarled Shelton. "You get your butt down to the woman's room and get her anesthetized and down to the operating room. I'll meet you there in fifteen minutes."

Travis, pushing a gurney, hurriedly went to Marigold's room. He propped the door open. The woman was stirring, but went still seconds after Travis injected her with a powerful anesthesia. She wouldn't wake up for many hours after the procedure was finished, that is, if she woke up at all. He gently placed her on the gurney and wheeled her out into the hallway to the elevator. In his haste, with his mind on that maniac's Shelton's timetable, Travis neglected to close the propped door.

CHAPTER 40

Andrew Copland had more than proven his skill as a helicopter pilot, and the Lynx had more than lived up to its reputation as the fastest copter in the world. At 1:55 a.m., the Lynx touched down on the helipad of the Center for Rejuvenation. The helipad was on one of low flat-topped buildings. They realized that the Feds would need this same helipad to land when they arrived, so they told Andrew Copland to get airborne and go to the nearest place where he would land and stand by. They would notify him if they needed him to come back, or they would give him the okay to return to Virginia. Gregg and Rick jumped down immediately; Rick took a moment to get his land legs back under him then they raced to a steel ladder leading to the ground. Once they were on the ground, both men checked their weapons as they raced toward the five-story building.

*****

Shelton Maxwell, Travis Mitchell, and Marigold Robbins were all unaware that the copter had landed. They were all in the improvised operating room, which was virtually soundproof. Marigold was heavily sedated and strapped to a gurney. Shelton—gloved, gowned, and masked—was seated on a stool next to the right side of her head. Over Travis's objections, he intended to do the final injection himself. It was only fitting that he be the one to take this historic step. He was proud of himself and could hardly contain his elation. Travis was busy hooking up the requisite instruments before he went into the cooler to retrieve the elixir, which he was sure would represent a lethal injection for Marigold Robbins. The digital clock on the wall read 2:10 a.m.

*****

Rick and Gregg made it to the building and found that the door was locked. They could see a security guard sitting inside with his back turned to them. They pounded on the door until they got his attention and held their shields up to the glass so that he could see that they were policeman. He opened the door; the men identified themselves and asked for directions to Shelton Maxwell's office. The guard seemed perplexed. He said he had never heard of a Shelton Maxwell. When Rick described him, the guard said they must mean Dr. Marshall, and that his office was in one of the one-story buildings, but he had living quarters on the third floor. It had not occurred to Rick and Gregg that the man was using an alias here where he thought he was safe. Marva Weiss had told them that Marigold was on the fourth floor so, after notifying the incoming feds of their plan of action, and warning the security guard not to let anyone know they were on the premises, they took the elevator up to the fourth floor. Halfway down the hall, they spotted a door that was propped open and cautiously approached with their weapons drawn. When they reached the door, they went in fast and low, one on each side of the door, in combat position. It turned out to be a suite of rooms, and they cleared each one, all empty, but they saw that the bed had obviously been slept in. In the closet, they found an overnight bag and a Coach purse fitting the description of Marigold Robbins's belongings, but no Marigold, and they had not a clue where to find her. Rick's gut was telling him that they did not have time to search every room in this place. Just then, Rick's cell phone vibrated. They had muted their phones, so that should they ring, the noise wouldn't alert Mitchell or Maxwell. It was the local authorities telling him they had just received a 911 call from a Marva Weiss. She said she was in this building on the third floor, room 315, and needed help. She was supposedly drugged by Shelton and was sure he was doing "something bad" to Mrs. Robbins that very minute. Gregg and Rick raced down to the third floor, entered room 315 with weapons still drawn, and found a very groggy Marva Weiss waiting for them. They had no idea that their entrance into the room had just set off an alarm. On the helipad, the FBI helicopter had just landed, and four agents jumped out, climbed to the ground, and raced toward the five-story building. One of them was EMT trained, and he had a bag of medical supplies slung across his back. With directions from Rick, two of the agents came inside, and took the elevator to the third floor where they joined the two policemen. The other two stayed outside to secure the perimeter.

*****

Travis handed the syringe to Shelton, who leaned over to inject his miracle into Marigold. He couldn't help savoring the moment. He whispered into the unconscious woman's ear, "At this minute, dear Marigold, I love you. I have never said this to anyone in life, but you are about to make a lifetime of dreams come to fruition for me. Thank you, dear Marigold, thank you." At that moment, an alarm sounded from the remote in his gown.

"What the hell ...?" muttered Travis. "What is that?"

Shelton, his face almost purple with rage, handed the syringe back to Travis, and with almost superhuman effort, he brought himself under control. "There is a small matter that I must take care of. It will delay the procedure only for a very few minutes. Return the dosage to the refrigerator until I return. If it is not still viable, you will pay with your life—and I mean that literally. Do you understand?"

Travis, grim-faced and shaking, nodded and placed the elixir back in the cooler. Shelton could not believe that Marva had woken up. He had given her enough tranquilizer to put down a horse. He would have to get back to his room and put the woman to sleep permanently. He had forgotten to relieve her of her cell phone, and he couldn't take the chance that she might be calling for help just as he was on the verge of culminat-

ing his life's work. "Damn that woman to hell," he muttered to himself as he started up the stairs.

*****

Rick was trying to question Marva to get a line on where Marigold was being held inside the building, but the woman was having a hard time staying awake. Whatever drug she been given was powerful. Rick dragged Marva into the bathroom and put her in the shower and turned the cold water on full force. He knew that they were working against time and that drastic measures were necessary. "Ow, ow, stop, stop, that's too cold," shouted Marva, but she was jolted awake.

"Ms. Weiss, you need to stay with us," said Gregg, can you tell us where Shelton took Marigold?"

"I don't know, I'm not a part of this, I didn't know what he was doing—please believe me, I don't want to go to jail," Marva wailed.

"We don't have time for this, Ms. Weiss, you need to get hold of yourself and try to concentrate," shouted Rick. Now, Marigold is not in her room. Do you have any idea where Shelton Maxwell took her?"

Marva looked confused. "Maxwell? But he said he name was Shelton Marshall. I don't understand."

"This is useless," said Gregg. "We're wasting time. Rick, let's you and I start on this floor and try every room, then work our way down floor by floor to one." He turned to the FBI agents. "You guys go up to four and five. Wait, hold on a minute. Call one of the agents downstairs. Have him ask the security guard how many rooms are occupied."

The agent listened on the phone for a minute, then said, "The guard said that only the two doctors live here. The other doctors come and go when they have patients, but only one patient—Dr. Marshall's patient—is currently in residence. The spa and kitchen staff and the building attendants are already gone. He did mention that Ms. Weiss here signed back in. He said that locked doors open with a remote device. He's sending one up by one of our agents.

Here's the elevator now." He retrieved the device from the agent and handed it to Rick.

"All right then," said Rick. "Let's go find Mrs. Robbins. Open every door in the damn place, and do it in a hurry."

Rick and Gregg headed down the hall, pointing the remote at every door on the third floor and then looking inside and clearing each room. They finished one side of the hall and started down the other side toward an exit sign, indicating a stairwell. They cleared the other side of the hall and opened the stairwell door and came face-to-face with a man who had just entered the stairwell from below. The man looked like the actor Terrance Harris. "Police, stay where you are Maxwell," bellowed Rick. With a look of incredulity on his face, the man raced back down the stairs with Rick and Gregg in hot pursuit. The two cops had been just as surprised to see Shelton as he was to see them, and unfortunately, they hesitated for the few seconds that it took for the man to turn and flee.

*****

Shelton knew he was in big trouble, but as always, he had devised a contingency plan. He ran down the stairway passing by the second floor and down to the first where he ran out the fire door, causing an alarm to blare. He could hear footsteps behind him, but he knew that all he had to do was make it to the small shed-like building across the parking lot, which was abutted up against the side of a mountain. Inside, he had discovered a hidden opening into what might have been a fallout shelter in the past. It led into an old mine shaft in the mountain. The mine shaft ran for a mile and came out at a place where Shelton had secreted the equipment and supplies he needed to make his way out of the mountains. Shelton was counting on it taking the cops a little time to discover the opening, which would be enough for him to make his escape. He made it across the parking lot and into the building just before his pursuers came through the fire door. He ran to the niche in the wall that marked the entrance to the tunnel, pushed hard on the wall next to it. The concrete slid back, creating a doorway. Shelton flew through it and the opening reclosed, leaving what appeared to be a seamless surface. He grabbed the torch sitting on the floor of the tunnel just inside the entrance. He knew the long-life batteries were good because he recently had replaced them. Without the torch, the tunnel was very dark.

*****

With weapons drawn, Rick and Gregg pursued Shelton down the stairs. They heard the alarm blare, indicating that the suspect had gone through the fire door. When they went through the door, they no longer had a visual on Shelton, and they had no idea which way the man had gone.

"He couldn't have run off into the mountains," said Rick. "And I don't hear a vehicle starting up. Let's try that shed over there." The two men ran over to the shed and went inside in combat position, one on either side of the door. There was no sign of Shelton.

"Damn," said Gregg, "where the hell did the guy go? Who is he, some kind of Houdini?" Rick got on his radio and apprised the feds of the situation and asked that two agents come to secure the shed. His main priority right now was to find Goldie. As soon as the two agents started across the parking, Rick and Gregg ran back into the building to continue their search for the woman. Back in the building, the two cops rushed up to the second floor, where Rick noticed a door at the end of the hall marked Authorized Personnel Only, and they decided to try that first. Rick pointed the remote device at the door, and nothing happened; there was no click to indicate that the lock had been disengaged. They were considering their next move when suddenly, the door opened from the inside, and a man in a white lab coat emerged. He was startled to see the men and tried to close the door.

"Police, don't move, get your hands up," yelled Gregg. The man compiled.

"Don't shoot, don't shoot," he pleaded.

"Where is Mrs. Robbins," asked Rick. "I want to know right now, and don't lie to me or I might forget that I'm a cop."

"She's just inside," said Travis. "You can see for yourself." Pushing Travis ahead of him, Rick followed the man into the operating room. Goldie was lying, unmoving on an operating table. Gregg rushed over and checked her pulse, and breathed a sigh of relief when he found it steady and strong. He got on the phone and radioed for the federal agent with the medical equipment.

"What's wrong with her, Travis," said Rick. "I assume that you are Travis Mitchell or Barnwell or whatever you're calling yourself these days."

"She's all right," said Travis. "Just heavily sedated. Look at her vital signs on the monitors, you can see for yourself. I didn't do anything to her, I was being forced to help that madman Shelton, he's the one you want."

"Yeah, and I've got some beachfront property in the dessert," said Rick. He took out a pair of handcuffs and snapped them on the man. "Travis, you are under arrest for kidnapping Mrs. Robbins and transporting her across state lines. You have the right to remain silent. Anything you say can and will be used against you in a court of law. You have the right to an attorney. If you cannot afford one, one will be appointed for you. Do understand these rights as I have recited them to you? You are in a world of trouble, my man. You are facing federal charges on the kidnapping. Now, if you want to waive your rights and talk to us, tell us why did you did it, and exactly what is going on here in this operating room, the feds might cut you a deal."

"I'm not saying another word to you," said Travis. "I want my lawyer."

CHAPTER 41

"Damn it to hell," ranted Shelton as he ran through the tunnel, cursing Travis and everybody else who had interfered with his work. Not only had he left his precious elixir behind, but all the written results of his previous research and experiments as well. No doubt the police would find the papers, and he was sure that Travis would start singing like a bird if he thought he could save his own neck, sniveling coward that he was. Shelton had the basic formula for the elixir in his head, so he knew that he would be able to start over, but all the results from years of perfecting the little nuances were gone. And he wasn't sure he'd ever find another candidate to receive his gift that he thought was as perfect as Mrs. Robbins. The madman was so enraged that he failed to notice all the dirt and little stones that had fallen from the ceiling onto the tunnel floor. Behind him, streams of dirt were seeping into the tunnel from several places overhead.

*****

Meanwhile, the federal agent who was a paramedic arrived in the operating room and examined Marigold. "I can see that her vitals are good," he said. "But I don't know what else I can tell you about her condition because I don't know what they gave her. Her pupils are equal and reactive, so I don't think she's in a coma or anything that severe. We really need to get her on the chopper and get her to the nearest medical facility so a doctor can do a workup to see what needs to be done for her." He looked into the refrigerator and confiscated all the vials of liquid that were stored there. They would need to be analyzed by the doctors at the medical facility. He used gloves to preserve any fingerprints that might have been on the vials. He also confiscated the "sharps" container and any empty syringes he found thrown in the trash.

Rick tried once again to get Travis to talk, but the man had clammed up. The paramedic transferred Marigold from the operating table to a stretcher and took her down to the waiting helicopter and loaded her on. The copter, with Goldie and the paramedic on board, took off heading for a nearby medical center. Rick and Gregg handed Travis off to one of the federal agents and headed back across the parking lot to join the agent who was guarding the shed where Shelton seemed to have vanished into thin air. They went inside to give the place closer scrutiny.

*****

Shelton was nearing the end of the tunnel; he was elated, he had eluded capture and was already planning how he could set up in a new location. He would have to find a new assistant, of course, but he didn't see that as a problem. Some people would do anything for money, and he had plenty of it, in plenty of untraceable accounts. He pulled up in shock when he reached the end of the tunnel. The exit was blocked by what appeared to be a huge mudslide.

"Oh, hell, oh hell, oh hell" he ranted. There was no other exit out of the tunnel. He had nothing that he could use to dig his way out, if that was even possible given the magnitude of the mudslide. He had only two options: stay in here and die of starvation and thirst, or go back to the shed. He turned around and headed back. There was a slim chance that the cops wouldn't find the entrance. Then all he had to do was stay in the tunnel for a day or two until they gave up and left. He could survive for a day or two without food and water. Shelton was halfway through the tunnel when suddenly, the ceiling ahead of him collapsed with a loud crash, sounding like a terrific boom of thunder. Shelton managed to jump back in time to avoid being hit with falling debris.

"No, No, No," he screamed as he slid to the floor in horrified disbelief. There was no way out; he was trapped, and if no one found him, he would die in here. For the first time ever in his memory, Shelton Maxwell succumbed to fear and collapsed in despair.

*****

Inside the shed, Rick and Gregg heard a loud rumbling sound, like thunder; but it seemed to be coming from inside one of the walls in the back of the room. Rick rushed to the back and ran his hands along the wall, and found the niche. When he pressed inward, the wall slid open, revealing a tunnel leading into the mountain. The air inside was filled with a cloud of dust and debris from an apparent collapse. That must have been the rumbling sound they had heard.

"If Shelton is in there, I think he's screwed," said Gregg.

Rick got on the radio and told the feds what had occurred. "I think we need a construction crew up here to see if we can dig out the tunnel. If the perp is still alive in there, he's in some deep crap."

CHAPTER 42

The feds contacted a construction crew, who told them it would be several hours before they could make their way up the mountain. While they were waiting, Gregg called the medical center where Marigold had been taken to check on her condition. He was told that she was showing signs of coming out of the sedation. Her vitals were still good. The material in the vials was being tested in the lab, but results were not yet in.

"It's time to call home," Gregg told Rick. "Mom and Maryann must be frantic by now."

When her cell phone rang and she saw that it was Gregg, Barbara was almost afraid to pick it up. Maryann looked frightened as well. Barbara listened intently for a moment, and tears began roll down her face. She gave Maryann a victory sign, so the young woman would know that they had found Goldie and she was still alive. After she hung up her cell, Barbara and Maryann hugged each other and thanked the Lord for His kindness and mercy.

"She's in a hospital right now," said Barbara. "Just so they can check her out, but Gregg says she seems to be all right. She's still under sedation, but she's gradually coming out of it. They haven't been able to talk to her yet, but they hope to do so soon. She's coming home, Maryann, we're going to get her back."

The construction crew showed up, and the foreman—a tall, muscular man named Jake—had a look inside the tunnel. "This looks like a real ticklish job," he told Rick and Gregg. I don't know how far this tunnel runs, and I can't tell how far the collapse extends, or if there are more collapses imminent. We'll get in there and start shoring it up from this end, but it's going to be slow going. I can't jeopardize the safety of my workers for one guy who may or may not still be alive. What was he doing in there anyway?" asked Jake.

"Trying to escape justice," said Rick. The guy's a kidnapper and a potential murder suspect."

"Well," said the foreman, "we're going to have to demolish this shed so I can get some heavy equipment in here to start digging once we get the tunnel shored up enough."

*****

Inside the tunnel, Shelton stood up and tried to assess how bad the collapse was. He shone his torch all around and saw nothing but huge pieces of debris blocking his way back to the shed. Soil and debris has also fallen on the path toward the exit blocked by the mudslide. Only the small section of tunnel he was sitting in was clear, but tiny trickles of dirt were still seeping in from above. Shelton knew that he had a limited amount of air. He was already feeling as if the air was getting thicker and harder to breathe. He looked at his watch and saw that he had been trapped for at least four hours. He listened as hard as he could, but he heard nothing to indicate that a rescue attempt was underway. He began to laugh hysterically at the irony of the situation. He was going to die in here—the genius who was on the verge of perfecting the secret of longevity. He was going to die in here and no one would ever know. He stopped laughing when he had the sudden thought that he was using up his air that much faster. He looked around to see if he could find a rock shard that was maybe sharp enough to use to slit his wrists. If the situation reached that point, he decided that he would end it himself rather than be subjected to a slow, horrible death by inches. He sat back down and tried to pray to a God that he had sworn he did not believe in.

*****

Unknown to Shelton, Jake and his crew were making slow, but sure progress toward reaching his location. They first had to shore up the walls and the ceilings then dig a little, use a backhoe to remove the debris, then do it all over again. They had managed to get about two hundred yards into the tunnel so far.

Rick and Gregg decided to turn the whole operation over to the feds at that point. Technically, since the case was a kidnapping where the victim had been transported across state lines, federal jurisdiction took precedence over the state. Travis had already been taken away in handcuffs. Marva Weiss had not yet been charged with a crime, but she was also taken into custody as a material witness. After conferring with the medical center where Marigold was recovering, the two Virginia cops called Andrew Copland to bring back his helicopter to give them a ride back home. Since Goldie had fully regained consciousness and had been cleared to leave the hospital, they would touch down on the way to pick her up.

Local authorities had interviewed Goldie, but except to say that Shelton kept her drugged and had once or twice injected her with something and kept babbling about her making his dreams come true, she couldn't tell them anything about the man's motives. The lab results had come back on the material in the vial, but medical personnel were perplexed; they could identify some elements in the liquid, but not all. There was a strange luminous substance that didn't match anything known to the lab techs. They did say that there was an element of toxicity in the liquid that would probably have caused irreparable harm to Mrs. Robbins had she been injected with the full contents of the vial.

*****

Inside the tunnel, Shelton's torch was growing dimmer, and he was terrified that he would soon be in the dark. His watch showed that he had been trapped for more than ten hours. His mouth and throat were dry; he was very thirsty. The air was getting worse; he knew so because he was developing a bad headache. For the past half hour or so, he thought that he had heard faint noises coming from the shed side of the tunnel. He hoped that he wasn't just imaging things and that rescuers were coming toward him. He no longer cared that he was going to be arrested. He just wanted to get out of that darkening pit of hell. Oxygen deprivation was making him feel very light-headed. Just then, he thought that he heard a sudden noise and saw a strange light emanating from the other end of his entrapment. The light seemed to be floating toward him.

"What the hell?" he said, as the light seemed to divide into shapes. Shelton was hallucinating, but he was certain that he was going mad when the shapes began to resemble two gray-headed old women, one of them dressed in rags with blood dripping from a head wound. Each of them held a syringe in her hands like a weapon, and they both were getting closer and closer to where Shelton was cowering with his hands over his eyes and screaming, "No, no, no, you're dead, don't touch me, don't touch me."

*****

It took the construction crew thirteen hours to reach Shelton's location in the tunnel. The federal agents rushed in to make sure that he was still alive and to take him into custody. Shelton was still alive, but he seemed unaware of their arrival. He didn't respond to either voice or touch. He seemed catatonic. They carried him out of the tunnel, and even when he got outside, Shelton did not react or speak. He had gone somewhere completely inside of himself. The mystery of what he had planned for Marigold was buried in there with him unless the feds could get Travis to talk.

CHAPTER

43

As soon as Gregg pulled up to the curb, Barbara and Maryann ran out to the car. They couldn't wait until he and Marigold got out and came into the house. Barbara and Maryann both grabbed Marigold and hugged and kissed her; all three women had tears streaming down their cheeks. They went into the house with their arms still around each other, not caring that it was hard to walk that way. Gregg followed them and wiped away a few stray tears from his own eyes. He carried in Marigold's designer purse and the rest of her belongings.

So much had happened from Friday to Monday. Barbara and Maryann had worried that they had lost a loved one forever. When he had found Marigold in that room lying so still in that bed, Gregg thought that his mother's fears had been realized. Even when she woke up, he was afraid that she had been altered in some irreparable way. Marigold had looked into the face of evil and had survived.

They had all made a new friend in Rick Williams, whose skill and perseverance is what brought Marigold home again. The things that they experienced from Friday to Monday had been life-changing for all of them. Maryann had begun to understand that her mother's need to be loved had survived beyond her father's death. Barbara had learned that adversity had strengthened rather than weakened her. She still loved her best friend with all her heart, but she had also learned that she could survive if the worst happened. They had learned from the feds that Travis had talked in exchange for a plea bargain that would land him in jail for only fifteen years instead of the maximum allowable for kidnapping. Shelton was still catatonic and had not uttered a word since the construction crew dug him out of the tunnel. No one had a clue as to what had pushed him over the abyss into total madness. Maybe he never had that far to fall in the first place.

Aftermath

After Marigold was returned home, she was understandably reluctant to venture away from home. Barbara came by every day and spoiled and coddled her for a couple of weeks. On Monday of the third week Barbara came in like gangbusters.

"Goldie, get up and get dressed. We are going shopping and then we're getting a manicure and a pedicure. Don't start shaking your head because I am not taking no for an answer."

Marigold could tell that Barbara was as serious as a heart attack, so she knew it would do no good to protest. Besides, she couldn't hide in the house for the rest of her life. She had not returned to her usual flamboyance, though, when it came to her appearance. She didn't even put on any makeup; she blamed herself and her vanity for allowing herself to be suckered in by Shelton.

They went to the beauty salon first; Marigold's stylist hugged and kissed her like she was a long-lost relative. She took Marigold over to the sink and shampooed her hair then toweled it dry.

"Miss Goldie, she chided, you've been cheating on me."

"Cheating on you, what do you mean?" asked Goldie.

"You had somebody else to color your hair." said the stylist. "You haven't been in here in a month, and I don't see a gray hair in your head. Usually, after two weeks, I have to give you your usual treatment."

Goldie asked for a mirror and looked for herself. Without her color treatment, Goldie normally had a ton of visible gray strands. She couldn't see even one gray hair on her head. And as she was peering into the mirror, she noticed that the whole network of fine lines that characterized her eyes were no longer visible even though she had not put on a speck of makeup. In fact, her whole face looked different, smoother, tighter, almost as if a facelift had been performed. The two friends looked at each other, and Barbara felt a little chill of something (fear or maybe horror) trickle up her spine. That man Travis had told the feds that Shelton thought that he had developed a fountain of youth serum and that he had injected some of it into Marigold.

No, thought Marigold as she continued to stare at her reflection in the mirror. *Shelton was just insane wasn't he, and such a thing as a serum that reverses aging is not really possible—is it?* (Had Marigold Robbins been able to see inside her own head at that very moment, she would have noticed a strange luminosity emanating from a tiny section of her brain.)

About the Author

Barbara A. Walker is a longtime Michigan resident. She has three adult children and many grandchildren. Barbara is an avid reader of books of many genres, but mystery novels always have been her first love. James Patterson, John Sanford, and Patricia Cornwell are among her favorite authors. Along with her daily coffee, she consumes several episodes of the police and mystery shows offered on cable television. After reading enough mystery novels to fill a library, Barbara decided to take the plunge and write one of her own. *The Methuselah Method* is her first offering for publication, but she has two other novels in the works. Barbara believes that writing is her true calling. She also writes poetry, skits, plays, and song lyrics. When she is not reading a new mystery novel, writing, or watching television, you often can find Barbara (and her muse) on the golf course.

CPSIA information can be obtained
at www.ICGtesting.com
Printed in the USA
FFHW02n1123021018
48655695-52640FF